Rude

Except for my shaking knees, I remained paralyzed. Nausea rose like mercury in a thermometer on a hot day. I was well on my way to losing that expensive dinner.

Then, as suddenly as it had come, the nausea receded, and through the haze that had briefly anesthetized my mind, my brain began sending messages. "Someone's killed Millie Larrabee in Meg's apartment! Get out! Get out! They might still be here!" I started moving toward the door.

"If they'd wanted to kill your friend, they'd have done it." Like the voice of Hamlet's father's ghost, Banion's words came to me. *Meg!* Where was Meg? I opened my mouth and cried her name. My legs, of their own volition, changed direction, propelling me into the bedroom.

I flipped on the light switch. There was a red splotch on the pillow.

"Oh, God! Meg!" I screamed. "Oh, God, oh God, please, please, Meg, be alive!"

Dell Books by Nancy Tesler

PINK BALLOONS AND OTHER DEADLY THINGS
SHARKS, JELLYFISH AND OTHER DEADLY THINGS

SHARKS, JELLYFISH

AND OTHER DEADLY THINGS

A MYSTERY NOVEL

NANCY TESLER

A Dell Book

Published by
Dell Publishing
a division of
Bantam Doubleday Dell Publishing Group, Inc.
1540 Broadway
New York, New York 10036

ISBN: 0-440-22409-8

Printed in the United States of America

Published simultaneously in Canada

May 1998

10 9 8 7 6 5 4 3 2 1
WCD

For Michael,
for always being there
and for being my most loyal fan

ACKNOWLEDGMENTS

My thanks to:

Jackie Farber, my editor,
Grace Morgan, my agent,
for their continued support, encouragement,
and wisdom

Kathy Lord, my copyeditor,
for her scrupulous attention to detail
and for keeping me honest

Ann Loring and the Roundtable Writing Group,
for friendship and the best kind of criticism

Marene Allison, former FBI agent
and V.P. of Loss Prevention and Safety for A&P,
for providing invaluable information

Bob Friedman, for being my bowling expert

Ken Tesler of Outerlimits Offshore
Powerboats, LTD,
for being a terrific son and a terrific source

and to

Bob, my legal eagle; Doug, my computer wizard;
Lisa, Noah, Karen, Leslie, and Leah,
for being my loving mainstays on the sometimes
rocky road

This novel is a work of fiction. Names, characters, places and incidents either are the product of the author's imagination or are used fictitiously. Any resemblance to actual persons, living or dead, events, or locales is entirely coincidental.

AUTHOR'S NOTE

The Key West Offshore World Championship race series normally takes place in early November. I have altered the dates to suit my own dramatic purposes.

CHRISTMAS USED TO BE my favorite time of the year. Technically, it's not even my holiday, but I've always been a sucker for all that fa-la-la-ing and tinsel and good-will-toward-men stuff. That is, until two years ago, when my ex, Rich-Sonofabitch-Burnham, chose Christmas Eve to fly the family coop. For the usual—a younger woman. Originality isn't one of Rich's strong suits. Neither is timing. Or cherishing unto death. Considering, though, that a couple of his cherished girl-friends ended up underwater and subsequently under-ground, I guess I'm lucky to have fallen out of favor.

Anyway, since then I've had a tough time staving off a sense of impending doom as the holidays approach. So I shouldn't have been surprised when on this Christmas Eve the malevolent winds of Christmas Past swept across my horizon.

The day had started out normally, innocuously. No ominous dreams had shattered my sleep the previous night; no ghostly apparitions hovered on the periphery of my consciousness. I'd roused Allie and Matt at nine and over breakfast shared in their excited chatter about the upcoming ski trip with their father. Then I'd seen them off on the bus for the annual middle-school sight-seeing trip into New York City, which this year included the Christmas show at Radio City Music Hall. I was in my office by ten-thirty. I was feeling upbeat about having made a tough-love decision to cut my favorite patient loose, despite my certainty that her initial reaction would be mild to severe panic. She outdid my expectations.

"I'll have a relapse!" she wailed. "I'll blow up like one of those Macy's parade balloons."

I refused to back down. "Ruth-Ann," I said unsympathetically, "the whole point of what we've been doing is so you can apply the techniques you've learned here to your life."

The limpid eyes filled. "But I have so much further to go."

"Oh, honey, look in the mirror."

"Vanity's against my religion," she said quite seriously, then giggled through her tears at my rolled eyes. Her midcalf-length skirt and high-collared navy blue blouse, required attire in her Orthodox Jewish circles, could only partially camouflage the voluptuous form they draped.

When Ruth-Ann first came to my office, she weighed a hundred and sixty-five pounds. At least fifty of them had settled in one amorphous blob above her waist, resulting in the almost total disappearance of any distinguishable features such as eyes, nose, and a mouth. Over the past several months, I'd watched in awe and delight as a soulful-eyed butterfly emerged from the cocoon. The shedding of all that blubber was accomplished through biofeedback brain-wave training, which allowed me to pinpoint the source of her eating disorder. To Ruth-Ann I'm a miracle worker, a female Moses. It's a flattering comparison, but I can't take that much credit.

As a biofeedback clinician, mostly what I do is relax stressed-out people. Give me a half hour, let me hook you up to my computer, and I can demonstrate all the destructive things stress does to your body, then teach you how to keep it from killing you. With another software program I brain-wave-train Attention Deficit Disorder kids and addictive personalities like Ruth-Ann.

I spent the rest of the session bringing her to a relaxed alpha state and filling her head with positive "self talk," stressing how proud she should be feeling at what she'd accomplished rather than the fact (vanity being a no-no) that she was undoubtedly going to be turning more than a few yarmulked heads. Hanukkah, I knew, would be the supreme test for her, so I threw in a little weight-control stuff, comparing matzoh balls (my grandmother should forgive me) to things shot out of a cannon and potato latkes to hockey pucks. My grand finale was a stern admonition. "You no longer allow anyone to influence your eating habits. You have learned to say no to 'Eat, bubbela'."

I'm terrific at mental tune-ups. Ruth-Ann left my office all smiles, her face lit up like one of those Christmas trees on the mall outside my building.

I hadn't scheduled anyone after Ruth-Ann because I was anxious to get home before Rich picked up the kids. He'd insisted they be ready at six-thirty to make a nine-ten flight out of Newark. I'd determined to let them go without even one crack to my ex about his predilection for cradle-robbing. Progress indeed. My New Year's resolutions were all about keeping my big mouth shut, the better to ward off the slings and arrows of outrageous ex-husbands.

Married for eighteen years, Rich and I were living a fairy-tale existence in a beautiful home in Alpine, New

Jersey. The fairy tale ended abruptly when the prince ran off with the wicked witch. So when the witch was found floating facedown in his (formerly our) swimming pool, I didn't exactly don sackcloth and ashes. Nor did I rend my garments when girlfriend/witch number two was found floating in her bathtub in the same condition. The "death by water" thing did shake me up, but panic didn't set in until fingers started pointing in my direction. Cop fingers. Fingers that had a detective by the name of Ted Brodsky attached to them.

Obviously, Lieutenant Brodsky's and my relationship didn't get off to a galloping start, what with his pointing fingers and my resentment (make that hysteria) at his considering me the prime suspect. But chemistry and the fact that the killer was caught in record time won out in the end. When you've been dumped and an attractive man comes on to you, every hormone in your body starts shrieking "Go for it." And Ted's a very attractive man. The monumental lust he inspires in me borders on the embarrassing. But for a variety of reasons we've decided to cool it.

It had been eleven days and four hours since we came to that decision, so I was surprised that evening, when I pulled into the driveway of the small brick house in Norwood, New Jersey, where my children and I now live, to see his shiny white Miata parked by the curb.

When I opened the front door, he was sitting in our combination family room–kitchen talking to the kids while alternately petting our monster dog, Horton, and Luciano, the dominant cat of our Siamese trio. Horty, who loves me more than anyone in the world, barely managed a tail-wag in greeting.

"Well, hi there," I said, as I concentrated on pulling

off my boots. "It must be Christmas. Santa's brought us a hot new car."

"In your dreams," he chuckled. "Just thought I'd drop by and wish the kids bon voyage."

"Oh. Nice."

Horty finally roused himself, meandered over to me, and planted a slurpy kiss on my hand.

Allie bounced to her feet. "D'ja remember the film?"

I extracted three rolls from my briefcase, for which I got a quick peck on the cheek.

"Gotta finish packing." And she flew out of the room.

I turned to my son. "Mattie, are you packed?"

"Pretty much."

"Won't cut it. Go finish."

He looked at me, troubled. "You're gonna be all alone on Christmas. One of us should stay home."

I felt a tug at the back of my eyes. Every so often one or the other of my children really gets me.

"We talked about that, sweetheart. How often do you and Allie get a chance to ski out west? I'll be okay."

"You sure?"

"I'm sure." I wasn't, but that was between me and my box of tissues. "I may decide to drive up to Worcester and see Grandpa and Eve."

"Maybe Ted'll go with you," he said, eyeing the man hopefully.

Ted smiled. "Better hurry, kiddo. You've only got fifteen minutes."

"Sorry about that," I said when we were alone. "He's a little confused about us."

"He's not the only one."

I wasn't going to touch that, not now anyway, so I made a big thing of greeting José and Placido, who were

5

having a wonderful time depositing Siamese cat fur all over my pant legs.

Ted let me go through the routine, waiting till I was ensconsed on the couch with a cat on each leg and one in my lap, and Horty weighing down my feet; then he leaned over and whispered in my ear. "Mattie's right. Animals or no animals, it sucks to be alone on Christmas."

"You have something else in mind?" I asked, concentrating on scratching behind the cats' ears.

"I'm hell-bent on seeing the tree in Rockefeller Center. Want to go with me?"

"On Christmas Day to Rockefeller Center?"

"Yeah."

I looked out the window and noticed how crispy clear the night had become, how bright and sparkling the stars. "It'll be a mob scene."

"Then maybe we'll just make a fire in my apartment and watch it on TV."

Was that the cats purring or was it me?

RICH PULLED UP PROMPTLY at six-thirty. Cheerfully, I told the kids to have a wonderful holiday and to be careful not to fall off the mountain. I blew them kisses till the car was out of sight.

Ted was on the phone ordering Chinese food when I came back into the house. In light of our recent pact, I was a little taken aback when after dinner, while we were listening to some angelic boy sopranos singing about the little town of Bethlehem, he pulled me close and kissed me.

"Very nice," I said, trying to ignore my elevating

heart rate. "But I'm not quite sure I know how we got here."

"It's our first Christmas together," he replied. "Peace-on-earth time. It struck me it's stupid to be making war."

"We just made plans for tomorrow. We aren't making war."

He grinned, nibbled my earlobe. "We aren't making love either. Though I'm open to changing that."

The kids were gone, we had the house to ourselves, and the offer was infinitely more attractive than anything I'd had planned for the evening. But I have this lousy problem with foot-in-mouth disease. "I thought we were taking time off to reassess."

"I've reassessed."

I twisted around to look at him. "Oh?"

"I came to the conclusion that if you're lucky enough to find someone you care about in this crazy world, and that person feels the same about you, why fuck it up analyzing it to death?"

By now he was caressing my thigh and working upward. I had to concentrate on hanging on to my train of thought.

"Because," I said, "there're things we need to work out."

He stopped doing all those nice things to my body. "Christ, Carrie, I'm not Rich. If you're going to let that rule your life—"

"That's not it," I said defensively.

"Fine. Then let's talk about what it is."

A sensitive subject that, knowing his history, I had never put into words. I fudged. "You know. We're both coming off failed relationships. Our emotions can't be trusted."

The scowl on his face told me I'd flunked the lie detector test.

"Psychobabble crap."

I started to protest, but he held up his hand.

"It's about my being a cop."

I flushed, tried the "best defense" defense. "That's ridiculous. I've never—"

"I know you've never." He got to his feet. "Carrie, sweetheart, I'm forty-five years old. I want a personal life. I'd like it to be with you, but I'm damned if I'm going to wait around for you to get your act together." He reached for his jacket.

Talk about not knowing how the hell we'd gotten here. "God, I only asked for a little time. We've only known each other seven months. Why all of a sudden are you—"

His voice was frost. "Because I haven't got time to waste."

Hell, I'm forty. Father Time wasn't exactly taking a nap for me either, but I had a problem. How could I tell him what I knew he'd heard once before—that I was scared to death that one day he'd walk out the door and never come home? How could I tell him I couldn't face another loss?

I couldn't. You don't tell a cop you're afraid to commit because you're terrified he's going to get his brains splattered all over the street. So I walked over to where he stood by the door and executed a female brushing-up-against-him kind of maneuver. "Come on. Peace-on-earth time. Why don't we just pretend this conversation never happened and pick up with the ear thing?"

He wasn't buying. "What's the point?"

"The point is we made a deal. All I'm asking is that

we don't do anything precipitous." I stood on tiptoe and nuzzled his neck.

"God forbid we should do anything like that," he muttered, but I could feel his body relent. "Why am I absolutely sure I'm being manipulated?"

"I can't imagine," I whispered, manipulatively snaking my arms around his neck and kissing the corner of his mouth. "Would you consider you were being manipulated if I told you right now I'd much rather make love than war?"

"I certainly would. You only want me for my body."

I pulled him down on the couch. "I cannot tell a lie. I'm crazy for your body."

"You're all talk."

I ran my tongue over his lips, my hands down his chest, over his rock-hard gut.

He didn't move. "Not bad, but you can do better."

A few minutes later our clothes were scattered on the floor and I was doing much better, when the phone rang.

"Shit," he said.

"Let it ring," I said.

The answering machine picked up. *"This is Carrie Carlin,"* the machine said. *"I'm not available to take your call right now."* I sure as hell wasn't. *Please leave a message after the beep and I'll get back to you.* Beep."

Meg's voice, hoarse, cracking. "Carrie, there's been . . . a terrible accident." A long pause, then in a whisper, "Pete's dead, and Kev's . . . they can't find Kev. Call me."

I was on my feet dashing for the phone, leaving my frustrated lover in a state of suspended animation.

Megan Reilly and I are connected by a bond much stronger than blood. Maybe once or twice in your life, if you're lucky, you meet someone who actually defines the word *friend*. I met Meg shortly after Rich left, at a time in my life when I thought things couldn't possibly get any worse. Then they got really rough. Meg took me and my troubles on when most people, except for the press, were avoiding me as though I were a leper with poison ivy.

Two weeks earlier she'd flown to Key West to be with her husband, Kevin, and his brother, Pete, who were there for the World Cup, the international offshore powerboat race. The boat had been designed by Kev and built at their new facility. A win at the World Cup would have put their fledgling company, Stargazer, on the powerboat map.

Meg's words resounded in my head like an echo in a canyon. When I got through to her, she spoke haltingly, almost as though she were translating in her head from another language. "Kev was . . . he and Pete were off Fury Dock testing it before the race. They had new engines . . . very powerful . . . supercharged. Something happened . . ."

I pushed the word out fast before the lump I felt forming closed my throat. "How—?"

A whisper. "Pete lost control. They're saying it was a heart attack. They recovered his body, but not Kev's—" Her voice broke. "Not Kev's." She took a breath that was more a sob, tried to steady her voice. "I'd gone along to get some photos, but I didn't stay. I went back to the hotel. *I didn't stay!* If I had, maybe . . ."

Thoughtlessly, cruelly, I bombarded her with futile questions. "Could Kev have been thrown clear? Didn't they always wear life jackets? Pete was only thirty-three. How could he have had a heart attack? Was the Coast Guard still searching or were they assuming Kev had . . ." I couldn't finish the thought, much less give it credibility by uttering the words. My knees gave way. "I'm coming," I said, and let the phone fall to the floor beside me.

When I could gather my thoughts, I called the airport and was lucky to find they'd had a cancellation for the following morning.

"Who's in charge of the investigation?" Ted asked, handing me my robe. "She give you a name?"

"I didn't ask. I wasn't thinking—"

"Never mind. I'll find out. What time's your flight?"

"Eleven forty-five."

"I'll drop you. What're you going to do about the menagerie?"

"I . . . I guess I'll call Ruth-Ann. She's off from school. I'm sure she'll stop by to feed the cats. I'll run Horty over to Dr. Stoner's kennel."

"He hates being caged. I'll keep him at my place."

I jumped at the offer. It's not easy finding a volunteer willing to feed a dog the size of a small elephant. "I'll reimburse you for his food."

"Don't worry about it."

"Meg said they haven't found any trace of Kev's . . . body."

"What do you mean? I thought you said the boat flipped. Wouldn't he've been . . ."

"I said *stuffed*."

"What's the difference?"

"It went in bow first. Pete'd had a heart attack. I don't know if it was before or after. Kev must've been thrown clear or gotten out somehow, but they haven't found him."

There was a pause. Then he said softly, "People disappear for all kinds of reasons, Carrie. Don't bury him yet."

The stone that was pressing on my heart shifted slightly. "What're you saying? You think there's a chance he's alive?"

"In my experience, bodies don't vanish."

"But it doesn't make any sense. Where would—"

"How much do you really know about Kevin Reilly, Carrie? I mean, aside from the fact that he just got out of jail."

The stone sank back. "I know what Meg told me. Kev wasn't involved in that fraud."

"He was chairman of the board."

"Pete falsified the data. Kev took the fall for him. Meg said he's always run interference for Pete."

Another pause. "Maybe he got tired of it."

I thought I'd heard him wrong. "What?"

Thunderous silence.

"What're you suggesting?"

"Nothing. Forget it. You want me to stay tonight?"

I let the inference drop, nodded.

He took my hand. "Come to bed. I'll rub your back."

He did, and then held me, stroking my hair till nearly dawn when I finally drifted off.

AN HOUR INTO THE flight the plane dipped, causing me to grab the armrests. I wasn't sure if we were over water yet, but I figured at some point before we landed we would be. As a result of the events of the past year, I've developed an almost pathological phobia about water. All summer I'd refused to swim in it or boat on it. Given a choice I'd travel by stagecoach rather than fly over it. Since I'd boarded American Airlines Flight 967 to Miami, I'd been chewing my fingernails to the knuckles and inhaling vodka martinis by the plastic cupful.

"Excuse me . . ."

At first I didn't realize the voice was addressing me.

"Are you all right?"

Puzzled, I glanced up at the gray-haired man wearing round rimless glasses who was leaning on a yellow-striped umbrella in the aisle next to my seat. He looked to be in his fifties, was wearing a rumpled, nondescript grayish suit, had a matching nondescript face as lined as the suit was rumpled.

"I'm fine," I said. *Get lost*, I thought.

He gestured toward my white knuckles. "My friend's the same way."

I fought to unclutch. "What way?"

"Afraid of flying."

"I love flying."

He smiled in a manner that said he didn't buy it but admired my gumption, and motioned to the empty seat next to me. "May I?"

I glanced around for the stewardess. The man appeared harmless enough, but I wasn't in a chatty mood.

His smile broadened. "This isn't a pickup, I assure you. You just looked like you could use someone to talk to till we land."

"I'm all right. Really." I turned my face away and stared out the window, spared from the view below by the aircraft leveling out. Somehow he took that as an invitation, and when I glanced back he was settling himself in the aisle seat next to me.

"She won't even get on a plane," he continued. "My friend, I mean. She took the Amtrak. We're going to Key West. I'm meeting her in Miami and we're driving down."

He shook his head. "I keep telling her. Stop worrying. When it's your time, it's your time."

It's not Kev's time, I thought stubbornly. Ted had planted the seed, and the thought had sprouted to full-blown conviction. I don't pretend to be psychic, but I'm intuitive, especially about people to whom I'm emotionally connected. When my Mattie was lying upside down in an overturned car a hundred miles away, I heard him calling me. I dreamed I saw Rich in bed with a faceless young blond, months before he owned up to his affair with Erica. Everyone has a sixth sense. Mine's probably more developed than most because alpha-theta brain-wave training, which I practice as well as teach, increases one's ability to tap into the subconscious mind. And something deep inside me now was telling me Kev wasn't dead.

"On vacation?" the man persisted.

"No," I said. "Visiting a friend."

"I'm combining business with pleasure."

I struggled to remain polite, a role model for my children, who weren't with me to notice. "What do you do?"

"I'm in boats."

My interest quickened. "My friend's husband builds high-performance powerboats. He's in Key West for the race. That's where I'm going. Maybe you know him? Kevin Reilly?"

A furrow added creases to his forehead. "Reilly. Doesn't ring a bell, and I know pretty much everybody in the business. He must be new."

"They were just starting out—he and his brother. They've already won some races though—the U.S. Offshore at Ocean City, Maryland, the National—" I stopped, my words calling up Pete's robustly alive face, causing my voice to crack.

"So you're going down for the races," the man went on, not picking up on my distress. "They're very exciting. I hear the competition's pretty stiff this year."

"I wouldn't know. Other than what my friend's told me, I don't know a thing about boats."

"Well, be prepared. It's not a sport for the squeamish. Someone always dies race week in Key West."

He said it casually, as if a life didn't much matter. As if it were all part of the game.

I twisted around in my seat to look at him. Had he heard about Pete? I was about to ask when he went on.

"Comes with the territory. Pretty rough people get their kicks playing with powerboats. Ever hear of Alex Diamantopoulos?"

I shook my head.

"Ask your friend who he was."

Was, meaning no longer among the living. Determined not to listen to a gruesome story about someone else getting killed in a boat race, I reached for my laptop, thinking I could discourage conversation and catch up on patient reports at the same time. Then I changed my mind, lay my head back against the headrest, and closed my eyes. Effectively shutting out my companion, I withdrew from my surroundings and put myself in my "safe place"—the treehouse my father had built for me when I was ten.

"Ladies and gentlemen, please return to your seats."

I opened my eyes, reluctantly drawn back to the present by the soft southern drawl coming over the speaker.

"The pilot has turned on the seat belt sign. Please make sure all

your belongings are safely stowed under the seat in front of you in preparation for landing."

". . . could give you a lift," my companion was saying. "Plenty of room in our car."

"Oh, no, thanks," I replied, reaching for my handbag. "I've already got my plane ticket, and my friend's made arrangements for someone to pick me up at the airport. But thanks anyway."

"My name's Banion . . . Simon Banion," he said, and paused.

"Carrie Carlin," I replied grudgingly.

"I've enjoyed talking to you. Perhaps while you're in town we could all meet for dinner one night."

NOT UNHAPPILY, I SAID good-bye to Mr. Banion in Miami and spent the next hour wandering around the huge airport, mentally kicking myself for not having thought to rent a car and drive to Key West. I put in a call to Meg, but there was no answer. I left a message on her machine telling her I was in Miami and would be in Key West by early evening. Then I called Rich's condo in Park City, thinking I should leave word where I was in case the children called home looking for me. In reality, I suddenly wanted to hear their voices. No answer. Just a machine, with a flutey voice. *"Rich and I are schussing the slopes with the kids. Leave a message."*

I didn't.

To keep myself from dwelling on that little tableau or thinking about what lay ahead, I called my dad.

Eve, his wife of only a few years, answered. "Dad's resting, Carrie. Is it important?"

"Not really. I just wanted to know how he's feeling and to let him know where I'll be over the holidays."

"Oh, you're getting away. That's nice."

"Well, it's not really a vacation. . . ."

Her voice took on a wary note. "What's the matter? You haven't . . . you're not . . . in trouble again?"

I've developed a kind of reputation with Eve—Calamity Jane. In a way, I can't say I blame her. It had to be a shock, reading in the newspaper that her stepdaughter was a murder suspect.

She and Dad met when he was in the hospital after his heart attack. It was love at first bedpan, or maybe it was the fourth. She was a gray lady, one of those volunteers who normally bring library books and juice to recuperating patients. When the aids went out on strike, the gray ladies stepped in and saved the day. Dad told me with great pride that Eve was magnificent, heading up the gray army like a benevolent sergeant. No bedpan went unemptied on her watch, no bell unanswered. When it was over, the hospital gave her an honorary certificate. Dad gave her his slightly damaged heart.

Gray lady hardly describes Eve. Except in the hospital, she wouldn't be caught dead in gray. She's just under five feet tall, pleasingly plump with frizzy ash-blond hair (courtesy of Lady Clairol), and is built like a capon—all chest. She wears pointy bras right out of the forties under a variety of brightly colored sweaters. I think she's what they used to call a sweater girl, who never got over it. I can't quite picture it—don't want to, really—but I have a sneaking suspicion she's hot stuff in bed. I do have to admit, if somewhat grudgingly, she takes superb care of Dad—hides his cigarettes, feeds him only organically grown vegetables out of her own garden, farm-grown salmon, and free-range chicken. Last time I talked to him he said in delight that he didn't know whether to cluck or spawn. Having been a widower for thirty-six years, though, he's loving it. Me, not quite so much, but that's probably because I'm jealous. I had Dad all to myself for a long time. But it's also because Eve considers it her God-given duty to protect him from anyone who might cause his heart to flutter. And lately I'm afraid that's been me.

"No, no. I'm on my way to Key West. Meg's husband was down here for the offshore powerboat race, and—"

"Oh, Key West is lovely. You'll have a wonderful time. Are the children with you?"

"No, they're in Utah with Rich, skiing. . . ."

"You lucky girl. I'll bet you're there with that sexy cop."

"No, I'm by myself. Meg's brother-in-law—"

"Oh, the hunk. I remember him. You watch yourself. Don't let him start up with you. He's the love 'em and leave 'em type." She giggled. "Or maybe you should. Give the cop a run for his money."

I decided to leave the boat unrocked. "Just wanted Dad to know where I am in case he happened to call the house."

"Yes, he'd've worried. He does worry so about you." She sighed as though she wished she could relieve him of that heavy burden.

"I'll call during the week. Give him my love."

Stuck with a two-hour layover, I decided to substitute food for love. I glanced around for a suitable place, settled on an open tropical blue-green food court decorated with genuine seashells and fake flamingos. The coconut palms were a toss-up, but the avocado and shrimp salad in the case looked fresh and Floridian, and I decided to eat heartily on the assumption it might be some time before I'd see food again. Balancing my tray in one hand and my laptop in the other, I searched for an empty table. Most I noticed were occupied by couples— young, old, and everything in between, all looking moony-eyed and romantic, which only added to my gloomy frame of mind.

They must put it in the water here, I thought meanly, as I squeezed into a space at a postage-stamp-size table locked between two others of equal dimensions. At one, a thirty-something, jeans-clad guy was reading a magazine while munching on a sandwich. An older man dressed in a loud shirt that matched the decor of the cafeteria was nursing a tall pink drink at the other. As I sawed away with a plastic knife at the hermetically sealed salad-dressing package, I had the sensation of being watched. From the corner of my eye I saw the younger man smiling, was about to—what the hell— return it and ask for help with the package, when I realized he was eyeing Mr. Rainbow Shirt. A minute later he picked up his tray, brushed past me as if I were Harvey, the invisible rabbit, and sat down at the other man's table.

Torn between pique and embarrassment, surrounded by all that ardor, I was reminded of Meg the day she left for Key West. She'd been so excited, so full of plans. Knowing Kev would be busy most of the time, she'd taken her camera, planning to take advantage of her surroundings. Ted and I had driven her to the airport. Later we'd laughed over the change that had come over tough-minded, level-headed Meg, overnight transformed into a giggling teenager in anticipation of a few weeks in paradise with her husband.

"Love can do that to a woman," I'd murmured,

squeezing Ted's hand. "She has him back after two terrible years."

"Let's hope he's everything she remembers," Ted, the cynic, had commented as we waved good-bye.

What had Ted meant? What had he meant when he'd said people disappear for all kinds of reasons? Did he think this was something other than a boating accident? I hadn't thought to ask on the way to the airport, and he hadn't volunteered anything. But he'd held my hand tightly as we walked to the gate and kissed me good-bye with a fervor reminiscent of our early days.

"Be careful," he'd said. "Call me as soon as you're settled." I'd promised, fighting the impulse to say, *"Come with me. I don't want to face this alone."*

"You finish, lady?"

The Latino man stood over me, poised like a stalking cat to pounce on my half-eaten salad and sweep it into a plastic bag. I checked my watch.

"Finished." I took a final swig of Coke, gathered up my carryons, and headed for Terminal E, where a bus waited to shuttle me to American Eagle Flight 5753.

The flight fulfilled my every nightmarish expectation. The eighteen-seater turboprop bounced around on the air currents like a child's kite on a windy day. I blocked out thoughts of the tiny craft plunging into the sea below by practicing deep-breathing and hand-warming exercises, ignoring the stares of my seatmate. I began psyching myself up with the kind of positive "self talk" I drum into my patients.

"So American Eagle's had a mishap, so what?" I mouthed softly. "Law of averages says lightning won't strike the same place twice. I can handle this. I'm cool. I'm calm."

My seatmate got up and moved across the aisle.

Mercifully, the flight was short. I'd been so internally focused, I was surprised to feel the plane touch down. I was still "self talking" away as we deplaned. *I'm strong now,* I told myself. *I can cope with anything. I'll help Meg get through this. If Kev's alive, we'll find him. If he isn't, I'm here for her.*

Ted's words rang in my ears, feeding my optimism. *Bodies don't vanish.* On the other hand, Ted thinks like a homicide cop, seeing foul play in the most innocent of events.

I don't have any particular hang-ups about thinking ill of the dead. Eulogies notwithstanding, a slime bucket in life doesn't become a saint when the coffin closes. Dead or alive, I'd hated Erica Vogel, Rich's intended. Actually, that's not quite true. I'd liked her considerably better dead. I hadn't hated Pete. I just hadn't particularly trusted him. He was a wheeler-dealer and a braggart, but handsome and sexy as hell, and brimming over with the kind of Irish charm that made you want to forgive his worst excesses. Away from his company, though, I would remind myself that he was responsible for two of the worst years of Meg and Kevin's lives. Meg had begged Kev not to go into business with him again, but Kev wouldn't be dissuaded. Pete was his brother, his blood. Case closed.

I made my way to the tiny baggage-claim area, familiar because I'd been here before, but under very different circumstances.

Several years back I'd come to Key West for a biofeedback seminar. Rich, then still my husband, had come with me, and we'd turned a business trip into a romantic interlude, frolicking in the surf and the hotel room like a couple of honeymooners. In those days, unaware of my ex's extracurricular activities, I'd treasured the moments away from home and office and had sneaked out of more lectures than I care to admit to indulge in both hand and body warming.

The airport was practically deserted. Amazingly, my luggage was first out on the turntable. All the doors in the terminal were open, and the warm sea breeze caressed my face like a maternal hand. I walked outside and looked around for anyone who might be looking for me. Meg had said only that I'd be picked up; she hadn't given a description and I hadn't thought to ask. Ten minutes later I was the only one from my flight still waiting. I was heading for a phone when a shiny pink taxicab pulled up next to me. The driver, a friendly, weight-lifting type wearing shorts, a smile, and a ponytail, jumped out and reached for my bag.

"Take you somewhere, lady?"

Pink cabs, palm trees, and friendly drivers. There's nothing to touch this at Newark Airport. I gave one last glance around and was digging in my purse searching for Meg's address when a hand reached out and took the bag from the driver.

"Carrie Carlin?"

I looked up and nearly drowned in the delft-blue eyes of a blond hunk whose ancestors could only have come from Scandinavia. His skin was sun-dyed a deep golden oak. He looked to be in his late thirties, was wearing denim cutoffs and a navy T-shirt over a body that would've sent Sly Stallone hightailing it back to the gym.

"Yes, I—"

"I'm Jonathan Olsen," the Viking said. "Meg asked me to bring you out to the house. I've been meeting every plane since four." He held out a callused hand. "I was on the phone with her just now when you landed. Almost missed you. Come on, I have a car."

Clutching my laptop, I followed the cute buns in the denim cutoffs to a brown Jeep Cherokee. The Jeep had seen better days, but I sank thankfully onto the worn seat as my suitcase was tossed into the back as though it weighed no more than my handbag. I waited till we were out on the highway before I asked the question that had been on my mind from the moment he identified himself.

"Have they found Kevin?"

"Not a trace."

I jumped on it. "But that's good news in a way. If—"

"It can take days for a body to wash up on shore," he said shortly. "Sometimes longer."

At the sharp intake of my breath, he softened his tone. "Sorry, but I think it's important you don't have any false hopes. And especially that you don't get Meg's hopes up."

My temperature rose, and it wasn't from the tropical climate. "There can be lots of reasons why someone disappears."

He made a right at a light onto South Roosevelt Boulevard and we were on Bertha Street heading into town before he answered me. "Any suggestions in this case?"

His tone was friendly, but I looked away, keeping my eyes on the pastel Victorian houses that lined the streets. I didn't want to elaborate on Ted's words or my own gut instincts to this stranger.

"Just a feeling," I mumbled finally.

"I was there," he said.

"You were there?"

"I pulled him out."

23

"Pete?" I asked stupidly.

He nodded.

"Then you must've seen what happened! You must've—"

"I was a distance away, underwater when the boat went in. When I got there he wasn't moving."

"You never saw Kev? Heard him shout? Nothing?"

He shook his head. "After I got Pete to shore, I went back. There wasn't anyone else in the water."

"But he'd have been wearing a life jacket and a helmet—"

"He should've been. But the sea was rough. If the tide carried him out . . ."

He didn't need to finish the sentence. Through the buzzing in my ears, his voice sounded far away.

"What was he like?" he asked.

"Pete?"

"Kevin."

I stared at him. "What do you mean? Weren't you a friend?"

"I never met him."

"Didn't you say he and Meg were—"

"I said she sent me to pick you up. I've known her only since the . . . accident."

Ted's words came back to me. *How much do you really know about Kevin Reilly, Carrie?*

I took my time answering. "I didn't know Kev well, but what I knew I liked. He was—is a very decent guy, loyal, smart. . . . He and Meg . . . fit together." When he didn't reply I looked at him and saw he was frowning. What was this guy's problem? "Did anyone else see what happened?" I asked.

"Like I said, it was rough that day. There weren't many boats out and everyone had left the beach."

"How come you were there?"

He picked up on the grain of suspicion I wasn't fully aware I was feeling and half-smiled. "I'm used to rough water. I'm a diver. I work the race. I was scuba diving that day."

A diver. One of those daredevils whose job it is to jump out of helicopters into deep, black water wherever there's trouble. I shuddered at the thought. Still, I supposed if anyone would have the know-how for a water rescue, it would be a diver.

We drove the rest of the trip in silence, curving in and out of narrow streets, all with look-alike picture-book houses nestled up against each other. It seemed odd to see Christmas lights sparkling in the windows while the scents and breezes of summer assailed my senses. Finally we pulled up in front of a small white gable-roofed bed and breakfast.

I saw Meg's slim figure before she saw us. She was sitting on an old-fashioned swing on the spindle-railed front porch, statue-still, her head in her hands. Her hair, normally a shining golden red, had dimmed to a dull facsimile of its former color and was pulled back into a knot. She was wearing jeans and a "Save the Rain Forests" T-shirt. My throat constricted as I recalled that she'd been wearing a shirt exactly like that the first day I met her.

I scrambled out of the Jeep and flew up the steps. "Meg," I whispered. "Meg honey, I'm here."

She wrapped her arms around me. I don't know how long we sat rocking back and forth, but at some point I became aware of Jonathan touching my arm.

"I brought sandwiches," he said gruffly. "She should eat something. You too," he added as an afterthought.

25

Meg straightened up and gave me a weak smile. "Sorry," she said. "Helluva greeting."

"Did us both good," I replied. "Let's go inside."

We went up to her little suite of rooms. Meg's magic was everywhere. A little Christmas tree stood in the corner, its branches laden with multicolored balls interspersed with tiny nautical ornaments. Even the tinsel was knotted to look like a sailor's line. Brightly wrapped presents lay scattered underneath its branches. Incongruously, splashes of tropical flowers, heads drooping now as though in mourning, peered at me from tabletops and shelves. Blown-up photographs—Meg's photos—replaced the bland pictures one usually finds in hotels, but these were not the melancholy photos of recent years. These were lively scenes, with Meg's unique feel for composition, but unlike anything I'd seen her do before. They were full of the joy of life, sailboats dressed in rainbow sheeting, seabirds in middive, sleek powerboats rising out of the turquoise water as though about to join the pelicans poised above them. And there was one of Kev in full racing gear, standing on the deck of a beauty of a boat with blue and silver stripes, pointing to the name, *The Megan*, inscribed across the hull. His face was lit with a broad grin, and he looked so dashing, so proud, so alive, I wondered how Meg could stand to look at the photograph.

"He loved racing," Meg murmured softly from behind me. "It's funny—you're always aware there's an element of danger when someone races, but you never really believe anything bad will happen."

The phone started ringing as we walked toward the bedroom. Meg jumped at the sound, but made no move to answer.

"Should I . . ." I looked at her questioningly.

"I don't want to talk to anyone," she said with uncharacteristic sharpness.

"But it might be—"

"The machine will pick up."

I glanced at Jonathan, who had started toward the phone, then at Meg's words shrugged and walked into the kitchenette. "I'll put the sandwiches out," he said.

"It might be Ted," I murmured tentatively.

"Get it then," Meg replied, and went into the bedroom.

It rang two more times before I picked up.

"Hello?"

There was a pause. And then a male voice said, "Kevin Reilly."

My heart started pumping blood into my throat. "Kevin is . . . he isn't here," I choked. "Who's calling, please?"

There was no reply. I spoke louder. "I'm a friend of the family. There's been an accident involving Mr. Reilly's brother. Can I give Mrs. Reilly a message?"

"Just have her tell him—"

"I told you, Mr. Reilly isn't available. His brother died in a boating accident several days ago."

"OC wants him to know it was a warning," the voice rasped.

I head a click.

Meg was standing in the doorway when I hung up. I turned my back to her so she couldn't see my shaking hands as I replaced the receiver.

"Was it Ted?" she asked.

"No," I said, turning back and making a superhuman effort to keep my voice level. "It was . . . someone said to tell you . . ." I stopped, glanced at Jonathan, who had appeared in the kitchen doorway.

"Said to tell me what? What?"

"Someone said to tell you . . . said to have you tell Kevin the accident was a . . . a warning."

The blood rushed from Meg's face. Jonathan was across the room in three strides, reaching out an arm to steady her. She shook him off and ran downstairs. He started after her, but I grabbed his arm. "Wait a minute. Wait a damned minute. What's going on?"

"There've been other calls," he said. "Night of the accident, Meg answered. Yesterday I took it, but I hung up when they asked for Kevin. Someone's playing games."

"T HREE CALLS," MEG SAID, her voice almost inaudible. "It means someone has reason to think Kev's alive."

Meg and I were gently rocking on the old wooden swing. Her color had returned with the help of the stiff drink Jonathan had brought her. We were both so emotionally drained that it was almost too much effort to keep the motion going. From the outside the scene was one of perfect tranquillity: the swing, cicadas chirping, a soft breeze rustling through the coconut palms, and the sweet smell of eucalyptus permeating the air. The ultimate "safe place." But I was feeling anything but safe.

"It means some pervert's read Peter's obit and is having his jollies at your expense," Jonathan retorted.

Stubbornly, Meg shook her head. "No."

"The guy said OC wanted Kev to get the warning. Who's OC?" I asked.

Meg looked blank, shrugged her shoulders. I looked

at Jonathan. The expression on his face was suddenly grim. "Who's OC, Jonathan?"

"I don't know."

I didn't believe him. I turned back to Meg. "The call you answered. What'd they say?"

"It made no sense. Something about a five-pin tap and going for a spare."

"Maybe it's a double entendre. Maybe if we can—"

"It doesn't matter," Meg replied. "Those calls tell me Kev's alive."

"What do the police think?" Silence. "You haven't told them?"

"She doesn't trust the cops on the case," Jonathan said.

"Why not? What happened?"

Meg stopped the swing with her foot and got up. "I'm tired. I'm going to bed." She walked into the house.

Jonathan rose, brushed the dried grass off his jeans, and started down the steps. "I'll stop by tomorrow."

"Wait a minute!" I shoved my feet into my sandals and followed him to the railing. "What happened with the cops?"

"One of them was obnoxious as hell. Meg was in shock when they broke the news. Told me she could hardly speak. He acted like she was hiding something."

"But, that's crazy. Under those circumstances, any-one would be—"

"Yeah, well, tell it to the marines." He kept walking and I followed, running to keep up.

"Kev was an excellent swimmer. You think he might have made it to shore?"

"Where is he, then? Why hasn't he called Meg?"

"Maybe he can't. Maybe somebody's holding him."

"You think he's being held for ransom? I like Meg's

photographs, but it's kind of a stretch to believe they'd bring in high enough numbers to warrant a kidnapping."

"What about the boat?"

"Mortgaged to the hilt. Meg told me."

"Well, maybe he's hurt," I said with waning conviction. "Maybe he has amnesia, but if he's alive, I know there's a damned good reason he hasn't let Meg know he's okay."

"Maybe he's running away from home," he muttered.

It was as though he'd slapped me. "What do you know that you're not telling me?"

He arrived at his Jeep, jerked open the door. "Nothing."

"There's something . . . what is it?" Suddenly I thought I knew. "That call. *You* took that other call."

When he turned, his face looked drawn, pinched. "Meg can't know."

"Why?"

"It wouldn't help her to know. You have to promise me."

"I won't tell her anything that would hurt her. I love her. You think I'd hurt her?"

I watched him get into the Jeep and start the motor, thought he was going to drive off.

"*Tell* me!"

"It was a woman." She said it was a go for New Year's Eve at Christopher House. That's a hotel in Old Town."

"A go?"

"Sounds like payoff time to me."

"But—but the other calls—they were threats."

"So somebody's getting screwed in the deal."

It was a few seconds till it penetrated. "What are you insinuating?" I whispered. "That Kevin's involved in something—that this was some kind of planned disappearance?"

"How the hell would I know? You knew him. I didn't."

"I told you about Kev. He isn't that kind of man."

"If Meg's right and he's alive, the guy swam ashore leaving his brother to drown. Was he that kind of man?"

II

. . . HREE, TWO, ONE, RELAX. And immediately you feel that warm, heavy feeling flow gently over you as you begin to visualize yourself now lying on a cloud, on the soft, downy surface of a cloud. And your body is completely and magically supported by the cloud, as you relax and begin floating—floating off into space . . ."

I watched Meg's eyes flutter, her breathing become more regular as the tension lines began to melt from around her eyes. I dropped my voice to just above a whisper, taking care to keep the same singsong rhythm in my speech.

"Imagine now a breeze, a warm, gentle breeze flowing down over you, taking with it all the tension, all the strain, all the pain—cradling you in a blanket of warming, soothing relaxation, allowing you to relax, causing you to relax and sink deeper and deeper into a deep and restful sleep."

I waited a minute, then rose from the rocking chair beside the bed, careful not to let it squeak, and tiptoed from the room.

Meg's a wonderful subject. Creative by nature, she's what we call an easy visualizer, but tonight it had taken me nearly an hour to quiet her. Considering the situation, I was amazed I'd had any success at all.

Curled up on an extremely uncloudlike mattress on the sofa bed in the living room, I couldn't stop my own mind chatter. I spent what seemed like hours alternating between counting the patches on the intricately designed, multicolored antique quilt hanging on the wall opposite and thinking about Jonathan Olsen's words. I couldn't get them out of my head. I couldn't get *him* out of my head. It seemed to me he was excessively concerned about Meg for a guy who'd just met her. Meg's a beautiful woman, tall and willowy with a milky complexion and almond-shaped eyes the color of the ocean off the Florida Keys on a sunny day. I've seen men—running the gamut from construction workers to college professors—act like moony-eyed adolescents over her. But even the most insensitive of them would hesitate to make moves on someone whose husband had just gone missing. Or maybe not. This is, after all, the anything-goes nineties.

At one-forty I decided to seek professional advice. The only professional I knew was over a thousand miles away, but I knew he'd be awake. His was a brain that never switched off before 2:00 A.M., one of those stalwarts who could do with five hours' sleep and be as sharp as a Wall Street tycoon for the remaining nineteen.

Ted answered on the first ring.

"Hi," I said.

"What are you doing up? I was going to call you in the morning."

"Couldn't sleep."

"What's going on?"

I told him about the phone calls, about Jonathan's

incredible theory, and about Meg's reluctance to talk to the police. He listened without interrupting. When I'd finished he muttered almost to himself, "They wouldn't have the results of the autopsy yet, I suppose."

"I don't think one was done. Meg hasn't mentioned—"

"They'd have been required to do a post. Unexpected death."

"Meg told me the paramedic on the ambulance thought he had a heart attack."

"There are ways to simulate heart attacks."

I was stunned. "What?"

"I don't like the sound of those calls. Meg should talk to the detective in charge there, be up front with him. He sounds on the ball to me. Name's Springer, by the way, Garson Springer."

As promised, Ted had been doing some checking. "You talked to him?"

"Briefly. For now the death's being treated as accidental due to natural causes."

For now. "What does he think about Kev?"

"Coast Guard's still searching the area. Apparently a body can be carried pretty far out by the tide."

"That's what Jonathan said."

"Convince Meg to tell Springer about the calls." His voice took on an edge. "The police aren't the enemy, you know."

"She knows that. She's just . . ." *wary*, was what I was thinking, but didn't say it. "She had a bad experience. We haven't really had a chance to talk about it. She's still in shock."

"Then you'll have to do the thinking for her for a while."

"That's what I'm here for." I waited for him to say he missed me.

"Carrie?"

"Yeah?"

"What's your impression of this Olsen guy?"

I couldn't resist. "Oh, my God, Ted, you should see him. What a hunk!"

"No kidding," he replied dryly.

"Yeah. Late thirties, six one-ish, blond, muscles like Schwarzenegger—"

"I wasn't asking for a physical description. I meant what's your impression of him as a person?"

"Oh," I said innocently. Then seriously, "He seems okay. Very concerned about Meg. Maybe overly much for a guy she's just met."

"Uh-huh. What's he do?"

"He's a diver. Works the races. He was there that day. He pulled Pete out." I hesitated, then said what had been nagging at me. "Apparently, he was the last one to see Pete alive."

There was a pause.

"You sure about that?"

"That's what he said. There wasn't anyone else on the beach."

"Interesting."

"Why?"

"Little puzzle piece. You never know which ones are going to help complete the picture. Let me know the results of the autopsy as soon as you know."

"Okay." I hated myself, but it slipped out. "Any chance you can make it down here for the funeral?"

"When is it?"

I hadn't a clue. "I'll ask Meg and let you know."

"It'll depend on when the M.E. releases the body, I suppose. Maybe I can find out."

"Okay."

"I'll see how fast I can wrap things up. Can't promise. I'll try."

I changed the subject to hide my disappointment. "How's Horty doing?"

"Doesn't miss you at all. He's planning to move in. By the way, I stopped by the house. Saw Ruth-Ann. She said the cats are all fine too. She's been taking them to her apartment at night."

"She's a doll."

His voice took on a teasing note. "I'll say. Haven't seen her since her Buddha days. Quite a looker since she slimmed down."

Retaliation for Jonathan Olsen. I ignored it. "You get to Rockefeller Center?"

"Not the kind of thing you want to do by yourself. It'll keep till you get back."

"Well," I said, feeling absurdly relieved, "guess I'd better not run up the phone bill. . . ."

"Right. Get Meg to go to the precinct with you tomorrow."

"I'll try." And then, without thinking, "Maybe I'll take a run over to this Christopher House—"

"No! Don't do that!"

Too late, I said quickly, "Okay, you're right. I promised Jonathan I wouldn't mention it to Meg anyway."

"Quit bullshitting me. I know you. Remember what happened last time you played detective."

How could I forget walking in on a dead body! Still, this was different. No danger of anything like that in this case.

"You hear what I'm saying, Carrie? Stay out of this."

Damn, it really bugs me when a man tells me what to do.

"I said I would," I purred as my hackles rose.

"I know what you *said*. This whole situation has a lousy smell. There could be trouble. It looks to me like Kevin and Peter were involved in something. Do me a personal favor and let the cops handle it. Keep your pretty nose out of it this time."

Why is it that when you finally meet a seemingly sensitive man who has the self-confidence and smarts to respect the female sex, he turns around and comes out with a condescending remark like that?

I yawned loudly. "You know, it just hit me how sleepy I am. I'll talk to you in a couple of days."

"Goddammit, Carrie, will you listen to me for once?"

"Night, Ted. Merry Christmas."

I hung up and went back to my quilt-gazing. Some tyrannized, male-dominated, eighteenth-century woman had sewn two hundred and forty-three patches onto the damned thing.

WHEN I KNOCKED ON Meg's door at seven-thirty the following morning, I found her sitting on the edge of her bed, looking like Garbo's Camille, as she attempted to untangle a rubber band from her mass of thick hair. Her eyes hadn't yet regained their luster, but there was a determination in them now, a spark, more like her old self.

I sat beside her. "Let me."

Handing me scissors, she said, "Just cut it out. I haven't combed my hair in three days."

Briefly mourning the desecration, I did as she requested. "Did you sleep?" I asked.

"Better than I have since . . . all this happened." She gave me a tentative smile. "Either my lack of sleep finally caught up with me or that stuff you do works."

"So I keep telling my insomniacs. Better than counting sheep." *Or quilt patches*, I thought. *I must begin to practice what I preach.* "Oh, by the way, Jonathan said to tell you he'll stop by this afternoon."

"I'll have to call him. We may not be back from town till late."

Relief swept over me. "You're going to tell the police about the calls, then?"

"I want to go down to the pier first, talk to some of the racers."

"The police aren't the enemy, Meg," I mumbled, embarrassed to be parroting Ted.

She raised an eyebrow. "That hasn't been my experience. And as I remember it wasn't yours."

"You're not a suspect like I was," I protested, "and you need their help."

"I'll think about it, okay? Get dressed if you want to come."

I got to my feet and gave her a quick hug. "Just give me ten minutes to shower and grab a cup of coffee."

"Take twenty. I'm going to wash my hair."

A good sign, I thought as I let the water run over my aching, sleep-deprived body. Meg was beginning to function normally. It'd make what lay ahead easier. I debated how much of my conversations with Jonathan and Ted to tell her. I'd promised Jonathan not to mention Christopher House, but despite Ted's admonitions I was determined to check the place out. If Kev had been there before, someone might remember him. Desk clerks and hotel maids could be bribed to give out information. Of course, I wasn't sure just how much information a ten spot or two—my limit—would buy me. Between the holidays, the kids' birthdays, and this little jaunt to Key West, I'd almost totally maxed out my credit cards.

As I ran a brush through my hair, I considered how I'd get to Christopher House without Meg questioning where I was going. Many of the hotels and rooming houses were within walking distance of Meg's B&B. The downtown area was cluttered with restaurants and shops, an endless array of places to pick up a map, which I planned to do as soon as possible so I could pinpoint the place.

I was putting the finishing touches on my make up—trying to cover the caverns under my eyes—when Meg walked in dressed in a blue sundress, her damp hair falling loose, a bright auburn curtain framing her pale face. She was carrying a cup of coffee in one hand and the phone in the other.

"Someone named Banion," she said, flashing me a puzzled look as she handed me the instrument. "Doesn't sound your type."

"Believe me, this is not my dream man." I whispered, wondering how the pesty guy had figured out where to call. Then I remembered I'd given him Kev's name. "I met him on the plane to Miami. He thought I was afraid of flying, appointed himself my psychiatrist."

"He was probably hitting on you and it went by you. Tell him you're taken. That is, if you and Ted are on this week."

"He wasn't hitting on me. He drove down from Miami with his girlfriend. He must be calling because he wants us to have dinner with them."

"Get rid of him and drink your coffee. I want to get

going." She placed the cup on the vanity and left the room.

I took a long drink of the steaming liquid before I pressed the TALK button. "Hello?"

"Ms. Carlin? Simon Banion here."

"Yes . . . uh . . . how are you?" How to shake this guy without being majorly rude?

"I'm very well. How was your flight?"

"Bumpy."

"Sorry to hear that. You should have come with us."

"Well . . ." I said after an uncomfortable pause, "I survived. Um . . . I'm just on my way out. Was there something you wanted?"

"I hope you won't feel I'm being intrusive, but I read about your friend's husband and his brother in the paper this morning. I wanted to offer my condolences."

"Thanks, I'll tell her." I reached for my shoes. "Uh . . . I really have to get—"

"Is your friend Megan Reilly, the photographer?"

I was taken aback. Was Meg that well-known? "She's a photographer, yes, but I don't think—"

"I saw her show in New York several years back. Brilliant work. Very impressive. I'd like to offer her my help."

I suppressed a groan. "Your help?"

"Yes, I . . . have connections," he said almost apologetically. "In the boat world, that is. I know people who know people. We could mount a search. . . ."

I almost laughed at the idea of this diffident little man and his pals in their motorboats putt-putting in and out of coves, getting in the way of the professionals. "I'm told the Coast Guard is doing everything possible, but thanks—"

"No, no, you don't understand. The police and the

Coast Guard can only do a limited search. They're confining themselves to only one area. I could mobilize many boats."

I was about to dismiss him out of hand when I recalled something I'd read about volunteers occasionally discovering things the police have missed. I should at least let Meg decide.

"Would you mind if I talked to my friend and called you back?"

"Of course. Or perhaps you would join my friend and me for dinner. We could discuss it then."

Persistent cuss. "I'm afraid we have a lot of things to attend to today, but maybe some other—"

"Suppose we make it late. After eight. That should give you plenty of time."

Annoyed, about to cut him off, I suddenly had a thought. "Mr. Banion, do you know a hotel called Christopher House?"

"Yes, it has an excellent restaurant. French. Would you like me to make a reservation there?"

If Meg objected I could drop her at home, but either way I'd get to Christopher House without having to discuss my reasons with her. I took the leap. "Fine."

"Eight-thirty?"

"Okay. And thanks for calling, Mr. Banion."

"Call me Simon."

"See you tonight, Simon."

I could almost see the funny little guy smiling.

"I'll look forward to it."

I DROPPED THE IDEA ON Meg as I was rinsing out my cup.

"Dinner? With a couple of strangers? I'm not up to it, Carrie."

"I just thought his idea about getting up a search—"

"The Coast Guard has enough to do without worrying about an amateur boat brigade in rough waters."

"They're not necessarily amateurs," I pointed out, carefully drying the cup and putting it in the cupboard. "Banion's in the business. He must know tons of people who've had their own boats for years. Maybe—"

"Leave the dishes," she said impatiently. "In the business, how?"

"I don't know exactly. Selling, I guess. Not in the manufacturing end."

"They're not going to find anything. Kev's not dead." She picked up her sweater. "You ready?"

Seeing the determined set of her shoulders, I dropped the subject. "All set," I said, and grabbed my handbag, thinking I had all day to persuade her.

As I opened the door, I came face to chest with one of the most intimidating figures I'd ever seen. Clad in a shapeless, multicolored shift that rode up on her massive hips, the woman was close to six feet and two hundred pounds. Her straggly brown-gray hair, in dire need of a cut and dye job, presided over a large, hooked nose and an expression that I think was meant to be agreeable but didn't quite make it.

"Mrs. Reilly?" she said, peering over the top of my head at Meg. "Coupla detectives downstairs for you."

Meg went white and reached out a hand to steady herself on the doorjamb.

"I don't like pourin' salt on nobody's wounds," the woman rasped, dumping salt all over Meg's. "You ain't responsible for this thing happened to your brother-in-law and your hubby, I know that, but it's bad for business

41

havin' cops 'round the place. I think you oughta start lookin' for another—"

I drew myself up to my full five foot three inches and held out my hand. "How do you do, Ms. . . ." I hesitated and waited for her to fill in the blank.

"*Mrs.* Larrabee. Mildred Larrabee. I manage the place."

"Carrie Carlin."

She took my extended hand reluctantly.

"I'm Mrs. Reilly's friend, down here to help out." I bestowed my most dazzling smile on her. "It's so nice of you to be concerned about Meg when most people would just turn their backs. The kindness of strangers," I added, doing a simpering Blanche Du Bois. "I don't know how to thank you."

She stared down at me, totally confused. "Well," she mumbled finally, "like I said, I know she didn't do nothin', but she's gonna hafta tell the cops she'll go down to the station if they wanna talk to her again."

"I certainly will mention that to them after we find out what they want." I lowered my voice. "I want you to know how much I appreciate your cooperation, and I'll certainly take care of you before we leave."

The woman stretched her lips into a smile that was more a grimace and stepped aside to let us pass. Bribery. Works every time. Like Scarlett, I'll worry about where to get the money tomorrow. I squeezed Meg's arm, and followed by the lumbering Mrs. Larrabee, we filed wordlessly down the stairs and into the small sitting room.

The two policemen looked as uncomfortable in the tiny pink and blue wicker-decorated room as a couple of lumberjacks at a debutante cotillion. They rose to their feet as we entered, and the older one—who was somewhere in his upper forties and had an oversized blond mustache that didn't match his brown hair—addressed Meg directly.

"Sorry to bother you again, Mrs. Reilly." He glanced at Mrs. Larrabee. "Somewhere we can talk to this lady privately?"

"S'pose you can stay here," she grunted ungraciously. "Not too long though. Can't guarantee nobody'll walk in on you. Maybe you should go up to her rooms."

When she'd gone, the detective looked at Meg and said, "Your call."

"This will be all right." Meg sat on the love seat, indicating I should sit next to her. She seemed composed, but I knew better.

The other detective walked over to the double doors and pulled them closed. He was shorter and squarer than the first one. His lips, lacking curve and softness, seemed almost a straight line bisecting his face, and he wore horn-rimmed glasses that reminded me of the geometry teacher I'd had in high school who told me I'd never get into college. I took an instant dislike to him. They were both wearing shirts open at the throat and loose cotton jackets covering what I assumed were their shoulder holsters. My eyes kept wandering to the first detective's mismatched mustache and hair. I wondered if he bleached the mustache, decided nobody would bother; it must be natural. Was he Garson Springer?

"Lieutenant Springer," he said to me as though I'd spoken. "That's Detective Hanover."

"This is my friend Carrie—Caroline Carlin," Meg said as she twisted the tissue she held in her hands into a tighter and tighter ball.

I could tell Springer recognized my name from his swift appraisal. He nodded at me and took the chair opposite Meg.

"Is there—" Despite her best effort Meg couldn't keep her voice steady. "Have you . . . found my husband?"

"No, ma'am. Not yet."

Meg's muscles relaxed—no news, in this case, being preferable to what she'd expected walking in here. I waited for her to bring up the subject of the phone calls, pressed her hand, silently urging her to do so, but Meg was more interested in what had brought the detectives to us.

"What's this about, then?" she asked.

Springer picked up a brown paper bag from the coffee table. "How large a crew did your husband's boat carry, Mrs. Reilly?"

"Two. The driver and the throttleman."

"Your husband was the driver?"

"No, that was Pete."

"They never carried a third crew member?"

"Not when they raced. The extra weight would slow them down." Her eyes fastened apprehensively on the bag. "What's that?"

Springer reached into the bag and pulled out a bright orange racing helmet.

"Was this your husband's helmet?"

Involuntarily, Meg's hand went to her heart. "Where . . . where did you find it?"

"It was floating not far from where the boat went in. It doesn't have the Stargazer logo, though, so it could've gone overboard from any boat in the area."

"Kev never bothered with the logo. It must be his." Meg's voice cracked with excitement. "Don't you understand what this means? He'd've pulled it off so he could see. It means he was alive when he hit the water!"

"Possibly, but keep in mind it doesn't mean he

would've made it to shore." Springer pulled a black and white checked cap with a red race flag imprinted on the front out of the bag. "This was found washed ashore about a mile from where the boat capsized. Was your husband wearing one of these?"

"He had one like it, but he wouldn't have worn it under his helmet. That could be anyone's. They sell them at the stalls on the pier."

My eyes studied Meg's face, but she seemed calmer now, as though the finding of the helmet confirmed what she'd been saying all along—Kev was alive.

Springer indicated the rim of the hat. "You recognize this?"

I leaned in to see what it was. Attached to the rim was a small gold pin in the shape of a powerboat. The enamel stripes on the boat were blue and silver. On the boat's hull was what looked like a tiny curved knife or sword with a jeweled handle.

Meg swallowed visibly. "I've never seen it," she said.

"The stripes on your husband's boat were blue and silver."

"Yes, but those are popular race colors. Many of the—"

"Hypothetically, assuming this is his hat and his pin, would you have any idea what the little knife might signify?"

The balled-up tissue slipped through Meg's fingers and dropped to the floor as she took the cap from Springer. She ran her index finger over the little pin several times before she replied, "It's . . . it looks like a machete . . . the knife."

A bell went off in my head.

"Would that have any particular meaning for your husband?"

"The boat model was called the Machete 42."

Hanover moved in closer, as if he hadn't quite caught Meg's words, crowding us. I felt claustrophobic, reminding me of the time I was a suspect in Erica's murder.

"You think he might've had a pin like that made up for good luck and neglected to mention it to you?"

"It's possible, but I can't imagine my husband spending time or money on something like that."

I jumped in. "Maybe it was Pete's. Pete wore a lot of gold jewelry."

Springer leaned forward in his chair. "That might be an explanation, except Peter Reilly was wearing a bandanna under his helmet."

"Pete always wore a bandanna on the boat," Meg said. She handed the hat back to Springer. "That knife could be a sword or a scimitar or some other implement. It's so small—hard to tell what it is exactly. I don't think it was Kevin's."

Detective Hanover spoke for the first time. He had a harsh, nasal voice that sounded more Ozarkian than Floridian. "What was your husband in the pen for, Mrs. Reilly?"

"If you're asking me that, you must know," Meg replied stiffly.

"That's so," he drawled. "But we'd kinda like to hear your version."

"There was fraud at a scientific lab he ran. He was held responsible."

"Wasn't it his brother, though, falsified the data?"

"He . . . yes."

"But your husband took the blame and went to jail. Why was that?"

"He was president. He was held responsible."

"Must've put a nasty strain on their relationship."

With a chill I remembered Ted's words. *"Maybe he got tired of it."*

"My husband loves his brother. He would never—"

"Excuse me," I snapped. "Are you implying that Kevin Reilly's disappearance has something to do with his brother's death? Because if you are, I think this conversation is over." I started to get to my feet. It's not a time of my life that I recall with joy, but I've had experience with law enforcement. I've learned a thing or two—the most important being, never let them see they've intimidated you.

"I'm afraid it might have everything to do with it." Springer turned to Meg. "Did you know one of your husband's jailmates in Danbury was a member of a crime family?"

Both men were pointedly not addressing me, but I was just warming up. "It's a prison, isn't it? Would you expect to find monks there?"

"Let me be clearer," Springer said. "There's evidence to suggest that Peter Reilly didn't die from a heart attack."

A little throbbing vein stood out like a scar on Meg's forehead. She reached up and pressed the heel of her hand against it as though to push it back into her head. "I don't understand," she whispered. "The paramedic said . . ."

Hanover bent over Meg's chair, his face inches from hers as he delivered the coup de grace. "That was a cursory examination. Our M.E. found a tiny puncture wound on your brother-in-law's leg, plus unusually high levels of potassium and myoglobin in his blood. There was also urine discoloration."

Meg opened her mouth, but nothing came out. I

forgot all about my decision to make mincemeat of these guys. "What does that mean?"

Seeing our total shock and confusion, Springer took over. "We've sent tissue samples to the reference lab in Willow Grove, Pennsylvania. They're equipped to do a specialized analysis. It will take some time, but it may give us some answers."

"Analysis of what?" I asked, seeing that Meg remained speechless. "What are you looking for?"

"Poison," Hanover said. The word hung in the air like a foul smell, like fumes from a garbage dump.

"Something that produces symptoms that mimic a heart attack," Springer added. "Something injectable that would have caused Peter Reilly to lose control of the boat."

"But there wasn't anyone else on the boat but Kev and Pete," Meg murmured, dazed.

There was a touch of sympathy in the lieutenant's eyes, none whatsoever in Detective Hanover's.

"No," Springer said, "it appears there wasn't."

The room was totally soundless. Even the insects seemed to have been struck dumb. I heard a low moan and looked up in time to see Meg's eyes roll up into her head. I made a grab for her, but she slipped through my grasp and slid off the couch into a crumpled heap on the floor.

CLUTCHING A WET TOWEL, Millie Larrabee barreled past the two detectives standing in the open doorway. Only Hanover's quick footwork saved him from being flattened. I wished he hadn't been quite so agile.

"I haven't eaten," Meg said weakly. "That's why . . ." She pushed away the glass of water I held to her mouth and struggled to a sitting position.

"That's only part of it." I glared at Hanover.

"Piss and corruption, I knew you should've gone upstairs. Shut those doors!" Millie hissed at the cops. "This ain't a hospital, and it ain't a police station. I'm runnin' a business." She made an attempt to put the towel on Meg's forehead. "The husband dead?" she stage-whispered.

"No." I took the towel from her hands and placed it behind Meg's neck. "They're still searching."

"So what the hell happened here? Whatsa matter with her?"

"Please," Meg said. "I just forgot to eat this morning. I'm all right now."

"No, you're not." I gave her a gentle shove back and walked over to the detectives. "You finished, or you planning on trying for a stroke?"

Hanover peered at me over his glasses as though I were a mosquito he would have liked to swat. "Listen, lady, this isn't being treated as death due to natural causes anymore. More likely what we got here is a homicide."

My skin went clammy.

"Homicide!" Mrs. Larrabee howled from across the room. "He say homicide?"

I turned my back on her and spoke softly through gritted teeth. "There is absolutely no evidence linking Kevin Reilly to his brother's death. You have no right coming here and upsetting his wife after what she's been through."

"Nobody's making accusations," Springer said mildly.

I'd heard that before.

He picked up the hat and dropped it back into the bag. "I'll count on you to have her at the precinct when we want her again. We've set up a command post at the Detention Center on Stock Island. She can get there by taxi."

I followed the men out. "I'd like to talk to the medical examiner."

"I'll be happy to fax his report to Lieutenant Brodsky."

"That won't be necessary. I'll take it to him myself when we go home."

Springer turned back. "Exactly when are you planning to do that?"

"As soon as you release the body and we bury Pete."

He shrugged. "You can go whenever you want, but Mrs. Reilly will have to stay here for a while."

"What for?"

"She was at the beach. She's a material witness."

"She didn't see . . . she'd left by the time—"

The screen door slammed shut.

"You can't do that!" I yelled in frustration. I hurried back to Meg. "They can't do that. They can't hold you. I'll talk to Ted. He'll—"

Meg's voice was barely audible. "I couldn't leave anyway, Carrie. Not till I know what's happened to Kev."

Mrs. Larrabee heaved herself up from the chair she'd dropped into on hearing the word *homicide*. "I got a little problem, ladies," she said. "I can't be havin' cops and reporters around. The place'll be crawlin' with 'em soon as they get their fangs into this story. You gotta move."

Terrific, I thought wearily. Where the hell would we go? Meg closed her eyes and turned her face away.

"Mrs. Larrabee," I wheedled, "you know the Pope couldn't get a hotel room in Key West during race week. You can't put us out."

She shook her head adamantly. "I gotta think about my other guests. If I let you people—"

"The reporters will be down at the dock talking to the other racers, believe me. Think of all the free publicity. Tourists'll be knocking down your doors to stay here."

"Yeah, 'xactly what I'm afraid of."

"You'll be full in the off-season when everyone else is crying for customers. Your employers will love you."

She hesitated. I could almost see her brain calculating the size of her bonus if my prediction proved correct. I pressed my advantage. "Of course, if you pass up the opportunity, they might not be so impressed. I'd sure hate to feel responsible for you losing your job."

The vases on the tables rattled as the landlady paced in little circles around the couch. She looked at Meg and then she looked at me. I smiled winningly.

"Probably gonna regret this," she growled, "but we'll see how it goes. If things get outta hand, though, you're history." And she stomped out of the room, pulling the doors shut behind her, the better to separate the pariahs from the general population.

"Well," I said, pleased with myself, "pin a gold star on me. My sales skills must be improving."

Meg didn't answer, made no sound at all, but when I glanced over I saw that her shoulders were shaking. I felt helpless. Kneeling by the couch, I stroked her back. After a minute she sat up, wiped her eyes, and spoke in an almost normal voice.

"Would you get me my cigarettes, please?"

I reached down for her bag and fished around till my

hand closed on the pack of Marlboros. I remembered she'd quit the day Kev was released from prison. Recalling my own love affair with wine during my separation and all that followed, I refrained from remarking on her relapse.

She drew one out, lit it, and took a long drag. "How could they think Kev had anything to do with what happened to Pete? He was his brother, all the family he had in the world. He loved him, he went to jail for him. . . ."

But I saw the fear and doubt on her face. I spoke forcefully, as much to reassure myself as her. "It was more than Pete deserved, but that kind of loyalty says something about the man. Doesn't it, Meg? Isn't that part of the reason you love him?" I searched her face, willing the old Meg—the strong, confident woman—to emerge from behind this unfamiliar mask of confusion. "You believed in me when you hardly knew me. Believe in him."

She allowed herself a wry smile. "Your sales skills *have* improved." The smile faded and she took another drag. "But what was he keeping from me, Carrie? I thought we had an honest relationship. I can deal with anything so long as I know what it is."

"Who says he was keeping anything from you? Hanover? The man's pond scum, a slug. Kev probably doesn't know any more about this than we do."

"If he's alive, why hasn't he let me know he's okay?"

"He has a reason. If those cops are right about how Pete died, Kev's in serious trouble. We don't know why, but wouldn't it be like him not to want to put you in danger by involving you?"

My own vehemence surprised me. I hadn't been aware till now that I saw Kevin Reilly in quite that way.

Convinced by my own pep talk, I began to construct

a plan of action. "Now, listen. This is what we're going to do. Tonight we'll meet Banion and arrange for his private flotilla to do some bush-beating. We can use all the help we can get." I gave her no opportunity to shoot down the suggestion. Enthusiastically, I grabbed her hand and pulled her to her feet. "Come on. Let's get some food into you, then we'll go down to the pier. Somebody down there must have seen or heard something. It's going to be up to us to ferret it out."

WE DIDN'T TALK MUCH on the way. Meg's answers came in monosyllables when I asked her questions about the layout of the town. All her energy seemed concentrated on getting where we were going without being run down by the hoards of laughing, raucous tourists who crowded the sidewalks. At the end of her block, I insisted we stop at a little grocery store, where I bought a map and she managed to swallow most of a half-pint of yogurt. I was relieved to see color creep back into her face.

As we drew closer to the marina, I could feel her tensing up. Never again would she approach this playground of the affluent without knots twisting her gut. As for me, despite my aversion to water, I couldn't fail to appreciate the view. The sea, a palette of frothy greens and blues and purples sprinkled with snowy sails and umbrellaed with seabirds, was most people's concept of heaven. Always the therapist, I took a mental photograph for use in future guided visualizations.

We passed a store window filled with boating paraphernalia and were crossing Southard Street when Meg suddenly straightened up and spoke in the clear, decisive manner I'd come to expect from her.

"Of course Kev would never hurt Pete, no matter what he did, no matter how mad he got at him."

I stopped in the middle of the street. "Kev was mad at Pete?"

"Annoyed. I meant annoyed. They had disagreements, over money usually, like most partners—how much Pete sank into the boat, on fancy gear, that kind of thing."

Several drivers honked in unison, and we sprinted for the sidewalk.

"That pin would've been Pete's idea of a public-relations gimmick," she said. "Forget the cost, pass them out by the dozens. . . ."

"Why didn't you tell Springer that?" I asked.

"I just thought of it. The stones must be glass, and Pete probably had the pins made up as a promotion."

"Where are the rest of them, then?"

"Maybe that one was a prototype. I'll go through their order sheets later. I bet I'll find an order for five hundred at least."

I kept my tone casual. "What else?"

"What do you mean?"

"What else is coming back to you? Did they . . . disagree about other things?"

She shrugged. "Kev didn't think much of some of the people Pete hung out with, but that was because he and Pete were so different. Pete was more . . . flamboyant."

It was on the tip of my tongue to remind Meg what she and Kev had suffered at Pete's hands, but she kept avoiding my eyes, so I traded the direct approach for a more tactful one. "Why didn't Kev like his friends?"

"They were . . . oh, you know the type—jet-setty, arrogant. But they were customers. Who else can afford a two-hundred-fifty-thousand-dollar toy? Pete was a salesman. He understood that scene better than Kev did."

Still walking a fine line, I asked, "Where was Pete while Kev was . . . what's he been doing for the last two years?"

"He was here in Florida mostly, raising money for the business." This time she couldn't keep the edge out of her voice. "He never visited Kev at Danbury, but he did have the capital to get them started by the time Kev got out."

"That'd be quite a chunk, wouldn't it? A business like this?"

"Pete could sell honey to a bee. He found backers."

No bees I know are in the market for honey. Substitute an *M* for the *H*—now, that's a different story. Where had Pete gotten the money to build these luxury powerboats? We were hardly talking about a mom-and-pop operation here. I knew Meg was asking herself questions she wished she'd asked Kev. One thing I've learned in my old age: Nobody gives you "nothin' for nothin.' " What had Pete promised his backers in return for their putting up capital? A piece of the business or . . . what? And who were the backers?

I moved to safer ground. "You said you went with them to watch the practice run."

Not safer. Meg's face clouded over as she recalled that fateful day. "I only took a few shots. It was overcast."

"Was there anybody else watching? Were there other boats?"

"There were a few people on the beach, but they left

when the wind started whipping up. The pleasure craft weren't out. The water was rough."

"If it was dangerous, why didn't Kev and Pete wait for better weather?"

"It wasn't really dangerous if you knew what you were doing. Not for amateurs, that's all."

I could tell Meg wanted to drop the subject, but I hung in. This was the most forthcoming she'd been since I'd arrived, and I wanted to get information while I could. "Jonathan was there."

"He's a professional."

"What do you know about him?"

"He's been terrific. I don't know what I'd've done without him before you got here."

"But doesn't it strike you as odd? The way . . ." I searched for the right words. "His concern for you. He's a stranger, really."

Her pace slowed, and she glanced at me in a manner that was faintly defensive. "I didn't want to question it. I just appreciated it." After a minute she added, "What has happened to us that we look for ulterior motives in every act of kindness?"

I shook off the sense of shame the question evoked. "Neither one of us can afford to be a babe in the woods anymore."

"I never was," she said sadly, "but every so often you need to trust someone."

"I'm not saying you might not be right about Jonathan. Just be careful, that's all."

We turned the corner and my attention was caught by an assemblage of tractor trailers and trucks parked under brightly striped awnings on a huge lot. Some had boats still attached, colorful, sleek, powerful—impressive even out of the water. Others stood free of their burdens.

"Wave to the guard like you belong here," Meg said. "I've only got one pass."

We started to cross Whitehead Street, approaching the little guard hut by the Truman Annex that led to the entranceway of the boat park. Suddenly a motorcycle zoomed around the corner and roared by, missing us by inches. We jumped back, ending up in a tangled heap on the grass. My ankle twisted painfully under me.

Furious, hurting, I yelled at the disappearing streak of smoke and dirt from flat out on the ground. "Asshole!"

Meg got shakily to her feet and reached out a hand to me. I took it and got up, gingerly testing my weight on the leg. The ankle held, and I hobbled over to a nearby bench.

"The idiot! He could've killed us." My heart was pounding. The immediate danger having passed, I had time to feel frightened.

Meg sat beside me, silent. I reached over and touched her hand. Ice. "You okay?"

"The motorcycle," she whispered. "It . . . did you see it?"

"You kidding? I didn't even hear it till it was practically on top of us."

"Kev has one just like it. Same make, same color, everything."

Shit, I thought, dismayed. *She's going to see Kevin in every store, around every corner, in every passing car now till they find him—or his body.*

"Kev's was a custom paint job," she went on. "He had it done at their facility. Blue and silver, to match *The Megan.*"

"Motorcycles all look alike to me. And this guy was going so fast . . ."

"You think I'm seeing what I want to see, don't you?"

"I think," I replied uncomfortably, "when you want something badly enough, the mind can play tricks."

The look she gave me was half-angry, half-hurt as she brushed the grass off her skirt and walked over to the booth. Limping, I followed, remembering to give the tall young security guard a halfhearted wave as Meg had instructed. I needn't have bothered.

"Gotta watch your toes around here, miss," he grinned, his eyes definitely not on her toes. "Race week the speed demons come outta the coconuts."

Meg managed a small smile, and we walked on through the milling crowds here to watch the practice runs. We passed stalls hawking T-shirts and sweatshirts shouting such catch phrases as *Offshore, America's Last Frontier,* booths festooned with brightly colored caps of the type Springer had shown us, and an endless array of carts offering edibles of every ethnic origin from hot dogs to lamb kabobs to egg rolls. Another time I might have enjoyed the sights, pigged out on the goodies, but not today, and not with the throbbing in my foot increasing with every step I took on the rocky unpaved road surface. Calling out to Meg, who had gone a few paces ahead, I knelt and loosened my sneaker, which in the last minutes had come alive and turned into a boa constrictor. I hobbled over to a row of white plastic chairs and collapsed into one of them. Meg retraced her steps and regarded my ballooning ankle in dismay.

"Why didn't you say something? You can't keep walking on that." Kneeling, she pressed gently on it.

"Ow," I yelled, as heads turned. "God, that hurts!"

"There's a first-aid station a few trailers down," a

plump woman behind a nearby book stall called out to Meg. "They got Ace bandages."

"I'll be right back," Meg warned. "Don't move."

Like dancing a jig was what I had in mind. I leaned back, closed my eyes, and took several slow, deep breaths, trying to deal with the stabbing messages of protest every time I shifted position.

"Great," I said aloud to no one in particular, "just what I need." How was I going to run around digging up information if I could barely walk? And there was tonight's dinner at Christopher House. No way was I going to postpone that.

"Here, honey, put your foot up on the bench. This'll take that swelling down." The motherly woman from the book stall was standing over me tendering a blue ice pack, the kind I keep in the freezer for Matt's soccer injuries. I did as instructed and was rewarded with almost instant anesthesia.

"Thank you," I said gratefully.

"Don't worry. Long as you didn't sprain it, the Ace'll fix you up."

I nudged a smile through my discomfort and thanked her again.

She handed me a folded-over magazine. "Take your mind off the pain till your friend gets back."

I thought about my *Streetcar* quote to Millie Larrabee. *"The kindness of strangers."* People did act strictly out of kindness sometimes. Maybe Meg was right about Jonathan Olsen. Maybe his interest in her wasn't sexual. Maybe it wasn't anything other than simple human compassion.

Yeah, and maybe the next time we run into Hanover he'll invite us to dinner, jeered the little voice in my head.

Within a few minutes the aching eased enough to

allow me to focus on my surroundings. Meg hadn't described who we were looking for. I had no way of telling the racers from the spectators. Occasionally I'd spot a going-to-fat, past-his-prime jock who I figured had finally made the money to own one of these pricey water toys, but most of the groups gathered around the various boats were young, in their late teens and twenties. Any one of the well-muscled guys with their suntanned grins would have looked at home on the deck of a powerboat.

After a while, bored with the beautiful people, I began flipping through the magazine. I remembered I'd missed the recent article on Stargazer Boats, Pete and Kev's company. Meg had told me a respected sportswriter had predicted a win here at the world championships. It would've been a tremendous boon to the struggling young businessmen. Trophies mean boosted sales, maybe even endorsements. Big money down the line. I was overcome with sadness knowing that there would be no trophy this week for Stargazer's Machete 42, that even if Kev were alive, he would probably never want to see another powerboat, much less race again.

There was nothing listed in the magazine table of contents about Stargazer, and after browsing through an article on thrills and spills in boat racing, I closed it. As I did, my eye was caught by the photograph on the cover: a flashy white offshore powerboat with black and silver graphics and the words *Diamond-in-the-Rough* splashed across the hull. It was accompanied by a bold headline and a color picture of a handsome man in his late forties with a mane of thick fair hair and dark, brooding eyes.

DIAMANTOPOULOS'S MURDER SOLVED, shrieked the headline.

When I was getting divorced everything I saw or

read seemed to be about infidelity. It was ironic now that *murder* jumped off the pages at me. I turned to the story.

DIAMANTOPOULOS'S KILLER ADMITS
TO MURDER FOR HIRE

A man police suspected of having murdered "Diamond-in-the-Rough" powerboat kingpin Alex Diamantopoulos in 1993 has confessed and struck a plea-bargain with prosecutors. Tony Kristal claims he was hired by organized-crime-connected drug dealers to kill Diamantopoulos in revenge for a deal gone sour. Already serving a sentence for racketeering and drug trafficking, Kristal pleaded no contest to a lesser charge of second-degree murder and was sentenced to twenty years to life in prison. He could have faced the death penalty.

Diamantopoulos was gunned down in a hail of bullets as he was coming out of his Coral Gables mansion on the way to his Thunder Row manufacturing facility in North Miami.

I closed the magazine and stared at the striking face of the man on the cover. A Greek Adonis. Alex Diamantopoulos. Where had I heard that name?

I was still working on it when Meg came back. The ice pack had reduced the swelling to the point where my ankle looked a little less like a blowfish under attack. Meg wound the Ace like a pro and I was able to walk, if somewhat haltingly, with my sneaker lace removed. While Meg went in search of a walking stick, I returned the ice pack and the magazine to the woman behind the book stall.

"Interesting article about Diamantopoulos," I said as I dropped the magazine on the counter. "Colorful character."

"Alex Diamantopoulos. Yeah. Playboy of the western world," she replied. "Made millions with his Diamond boats. Hobnobbed with all the biggies. You know, politicians, celebs, all the rich and famous."

"No kidding. Like who?"

She laughed. "You won't hear any names from me. You'd know 'em though. He sold plenty of them their boats. Took 'em on joy rides, gave parties like you wouldn't believe."

I looked suitably impressed. "Looks like all his powerful friends couldn't put Humpty Dumpty together again, though."

"Yeah, well, the rich and powerful weren't his only buddies. Ya don't cross the mob. Not if you want to go on breathin'.".

She turned to help a customer and I went back and sat on the hard plastic chair, my mind in turmoil. Snatches of conversations were coming back to me, Ted's puzzle pieces beginning to form a sinister picture. I remembered where I'd heard the name Diamantopoulos. Banion had mentioned him on the plane. Something about rough people being involved with powerboats. Kristal had been hired by organized-crime-connected drug dealers. Could Banion have meant organized crime . . . *Mafia* . . . when he referred to "rough people"? Organized crime. OC! My heart skipped about five hundred beats. "OC wants him to know it was a warning." Diamantopoulos's arresting face flashed across the screen of my mind. *Diamond-in-the-Rough kingpin, Alex Diamantopoulos.* Kingpin because he ruled the industry? Or . . . did kingpin allude to something else? A kingpin was also the central pin in a bowling setup. I hadn't bowled since I was sixteen when I took it in gym to avoid getting all disgusting and sweated up running track, but I thought I remembered some of the lingo. A strike was when you knocked down all the pins with one ball, which I'd never managed to do. A spare was when you got the rest of them with the second ball, something I rarely did. A ten-pin tap . . . I think that was when the tenth pin was left standing. What was it the woman on the phone had said to Meg? "A five-pin tap and going for a spare." A five-pin tap, then, would be when the *fifth* pin was left standing. The fifth pin. The central pin. The kingpin. So in bowling parlance a five-pin tap would mean the central pin had been left standing after the other pins had been knocked down, and going for a spare would mean the second ball would take the kingpin out!

"Ya don't cross the mob," the book lady had said. According to the article, Diamantopoulos had crossed the mob. Could the money for Stargazer have been *mob* money? Had Pete cheated the Mafia and paid with his life? Did these riddles mean that Kevin had survived but was on some kind of hit list? Suddenly, sitting on that plastic chair, basking in the soothing Florida sunshine, I was more terrified than I'd been since the day I'd found Rich's secretary's lacerated body floating in her bathtub.

Meg returned a few minutes later waving a short metal pole.

"Looks like a broken tent pole," I joked, trying to cover my anxiety.

"It is. Best I could do."

I attempted a few steps. "It's fine. Thanks. Thanks again," I called out to the magazine lady.

"Don't mention it. Have fun."

As we walked down to the pier I must have been making little gasping noises, because Meg cast a worried look in my direction. "You okay? Can you manage on that foot?"

"Yeah," I said, mopping my forehead with a tissue. "I'm just hot. It must be in the eighties by now."

It was, so Meg accepted my excuse, her eyes sweeping the basin in search of her objectives. I followed her gaze to where a group of girls were flirting with the driver of a racy fire-engine-red boat with a sunburst logo on the hull.

"That's Greg Silver's boat," she said. "He and Pete were friends, knew each other from their old Thunder Row days."

The name jolted me. "What did you say?"

"I said, that's Greg—"

"No, no, about Thunder Row."

"I said Pete and Greg knew each other from when they both worked on Thunder Row. That's a street in North Miami where all the 'go-fast' boats used to be built."

"When did Pete work there?" I asked.

"Years ago. When he got out of college. Kev did too, the following year. That's when they really got interested in high-performance boats. Never followed up on it, though, till they were drummed out of the pharmaceutical business."

11

. . . COULDN'T BELIEVE IT WHEN I heard. Can't tell you how awful we all feel." The curly-headed young man in his late twenties was wearing khaki cutoffs and a red shirt with the sunburst logo on the pocket. Standing in the cockpit busily scrubbing the interior, he was having a difficult time looking at Meg— not a usual affliction for men of any age.

"Pete and Kev had the best boat in the Open Class. I heard it was some kind of new design. Ultralight and strong, with a ventilated bottom. Great engines."

"The design was Kev's," Meg said to me, unable to mask either her pain or her pride in her husband's accomplishment. "It's what kept him sane during the past couple of years."

"They were a cinch to take first. Ask anyone. Nobody would've got close." Silver shook his head. "Always a risk. We all know that. But a heart attack. Jesus! He was young. Who would think . . ."

Obviously, the cops hadn't spread the word. No one seemed to be questioning the heart-attack story.

"Have you been down here all week, Greg?" Meg inquired.

"Drove down from Virginia on Monday."

"Did Pete and Kev seem okay? I mean, they didn't seem especially worried about anything, did they?"

"You kidding? Kev was on a high, like he knew they had this one wrapped up. But I figured you being here had something to do with it. It wasn't just about winning." He looked at Meg then. "He was crazy for you, Meg. He had your picture taped to the dashboard."

Meg's face twisted. "I know," she replied. "I don't believe he's dead, Greg."

Stunned, his eyes swiveled from one to the other of us. "Oh, Christ," he groaned. "Meg, there's no way . . . I mean, I heard . . ." His face turned bright red through his tan, and his eyes sought mine, as if asking my help with this deranged woman.

I repeated what Meg had said, not knowing what else to do. "They haven't found his body, so the possibility exists he made it to shore. We're investigation every avenue . . ." Lamely, my voice trailed off.

"But that's . . . okay, if he's alive, where is he?"

The million-dollar question.

"Meg feels," I replied, "that Kev may be hurt, or in

some sort of trouble. We were hoping one of his or Pete's friends might know something that would help us find him."

"Know *what*? It wouldn't make any sense—" He stopped. "Look, why don't you talk to Stu Kellerman?" He indicated a mop of red hair sticking up out of the cockpit of a yellow powerboat sporting orange stripes and a huge black panther on its hull. "He and Pete were pretty tight. Maybe he knows something."

"Kellerman?" Meg repeated. "I never heard that name."

Greg shrugged. "Could be I'm wrong. I don't live down here. I just saw Pete and Stu drinkin' at Barefoot Bob's a coupla times, so I kinda assumed . . ."

"You know him?" Meg asked.

"Not too well."

Something in his tone made me look at him closely. "Don't you like him?"

"Like I said, I don't know him real well. He's new on the circuit."

It was clear he had nothing more to tell us, so we thanked him and left him looking morose even after the admiring gaggle of girls resurrounded him.

"Mr. Kellerman," Meg called out as we headed for the slip where the yellow boat was docked. "It's Meg Reilly. Could I talk to you, please?"

The red mop disappeared, and a few seconds later I saw its owner, a bare-chested string bean of a guy, untying the ropes that secured the boat to the dock. The engine sprang to life, and the black panther charged out into the bay. Meg ran ahead waving and calling. I followed as quickly as my ankle would permit, but the boat picked up speed, cutting through the water, creating a wake that set several of the other craft to rocking dangerously.

"Hey, asshole," someone shouted. "There's a speed limit in the fuckin' harbor!"

Kellerman never glanced back.

"That was weird," I said. "I could've sworn he saw you."

"I think talking to me makes people uncomfortable," Meg murmured. "They think the bad luck'll rub off. We'll have to catch him tomorrow." And she turned and headed down to the boat in the next slip.

I didn't follow right away. I stood watching the man in the yellow boat get smaller and smaller. I wouldn't swear to it, but I thought I saw him look back at me and raise his hand in an obscene gesture. But maybe he was just waving.

We spent the rest of the afternoon chasing down several more race drivers, none of whom had anything useful to add. Everyone had been shocked and saddened by the news and was genuinely sympathetic to Meg. Kev and Pete had been well-liked. If there was an undercurrent of relief that hopes for victory had improved with the withdrawal of the Machete 42, guilt made them cover it well. Meg thanked them graciously for their concern, but I could feel her discouragement, see it in the slump of her shoulders as we walked back.

At the foot of Duval Street, we decided to take a taxi to spare my ankle. That's when I discovered that those pretty pink cabs in Key West are no easier to come by at 5:00 P.M. than the big yellow ones in New York City.

"Need a lift?" The invitation came from a brown Jeep Cherokee pulling up across the street. The Viking to the rescue. I have to admit I was glad to see him.

"What happened to you?" he inquired as I attempted to scramble up the suddenly insurmountable step into the back of the Jeep. He was out of the car and I was lifted and unceremoniously dumped onto the seat like one of those twenty-five-pound sacks of kitty litter I'm always buying.

"Twisted my ankle," I grunted, tugging at my shorts, trying to settle myself around the paraphernalia that took up most of the seat. Meg climbed into the passenger seat.

"How'd you do that?"

"We went down to the pier and I—"

"She tripped over one of the boat trailers," Meg interrupted.

If Meg didn't want to mention the motorcycle to Jonathan, it was okay with me.

He shot a curious glance in her direction, but didn't pursue it. A few minutes later we turned a corner and pulled up in front of a small sand-colored house with a Spanish tiled roof and orange-brown shutters on the windows. The veranda was encased in lush tropical foliage that crept up the railing so only portions of it were visible from the street.

"How about a drink to anesthetize the pain?" he asked, twisting around and directing the question to me.

"Where are we?"

"My place." He turned back to Meg. "Want to show you something."

I was about to make an excuse about wanting to ice my ankle, which I did, when Meg said, "Fine."

"Fine," I grumbled. Getting out of the Jeep was easier than getting in, and I lowered myself carefully to the ground before Jonathan had a chance to throw me over his shoulder and haul me up to his lair.

As soon as he opened the door and we walked down the little hallway to his living room, it was stunningly obvious why he'd brought us here. Water-phobic me immediately felt seasick.

Occupying one entire wall of the room was a giant marine-reef aquarium swarming with gyrating life of every shape, color, and description. There were speckled fish and striped ones, spotted fish and fish with patches, little ones, middle-sized ones, fish that looked like horses and fish that resembled lions, and even fish with eyes on both their heads and tails so you literally couldn't tell which end was up, all darting in and out of delicately hued coral and swaying ferns. Every one of them looked as though some artist on LSD had gone wild with paintbrush and palette. I sank down on the couch, trying not to look at the sloshing water.

"It's spectacular," Meg gasped.

"Um, incredible," I murmured as the water sloshed against the glass. I fussed with my bandaged ankle, waiting for the dizziness to pass.

When I raised my eyes, two matching bright green fish with dark aqua and lemon circular patches and tails that looked like iridescent fans swam right up to the clear wall and blinked at me.

"They're positively psychedelic," I muttered.

Jonathan nodded approvingly, as though I'd said something brilliant. "Those actually *are* called psychedelic fish."

"You're joking."

"I'm not. Scientific name, *Synchiropus picturatus.* This little guy here," he went on, referring to a much gaudier version symmetrically splashed with reds and blues and greens, "is a mandarin fish. Same species, but his mucous skin is poisonous."

"You mean if another fish touches it, it'll die?"

"Nature's way. It's how it defends itself."

"You should market them," I commented dryly. "Better than an attack dog."

Jonathan laughed. "I'm a marine biologist. It's my passion. I've been collecting these little guys for years."

Meg indicated an almost rectangular-shaped yellow-brown flash with royal stripes rippling diagonally up his body. "What's that one?"

"Jojo's an angelfish," he said. "I've had him since he was a juvenile."

I stared at him. "Jojo? You name them?"

He smiled, his usually somber face transformed by his enthusiasm for his subject. "Guilty."

Now, what do you make of a guy who jumps out of helicopters, but names his fish?

"He's getting a bit difficult to keep now, though," he went on. "I might have to separate him."

"Why?" Meg asked.

"Angelfish get destructive with age."

"I know people like that," I said.

"I assume this one's kept separate for the same reason?" Meg said from the other end of the room. "I'd sure hate to meet him in a dark alley."

Jonathan moved over to where Meg stood peering into a partitioned section of the tank. I followed to where I could just see the top half of a snakelike creature, patterned and colored like a giraffe, poking its head out of a rocky cave. It had the ugliest, meanest face I've ever seen.

"Snowy's a snowflake moray eel. Jojo and his housemates wouldn't survive long with him as a tank companion. Even I have to be careful when I feed him. He's got kind of a nasty bite."

Now, I'm an animal lover. I'm crazy about my shaggy mongrel dog and my three cats. I hug and kiss them. I sleep with them. I have a friend who has a pig named Sizzie, which started out little and cute and pink and ended up covered with coarse black hair and a huge belly that drags on the ground, and I can even relate to her affection for him. But what kind of a wacko has an eel for a pet? "Must get your sheets a little damp when you cuddle in bed."

"He's a magnificent specimen. Look at his markings. Beautiful."

I thought I'd appreciate those markings infinitely more on a pair of shoes, but refrained from saying it.

"The Romans prized eels highly, you know," he continued. "Used to deck them out with jewels."

"My ex-husband prizes piranhas highly," I remarked. "He decks them out with jewels. Mostly mine."

Jonathan looked at me as though I'd suddenly started talking Swahili.

"Private joke," Meg laughed. "Carrie's ex-husband got half her jewelry in the divorce."

"Ah." He eyed me sympathetically. "Men are pigs."

"Well, not all of them," I conceded, thinking of Ted and my son. And with Sizzie in mind I said, "Anyway, I like pigs."

"These eels had other uses."

"Broiled, on toast?"

He grinned. "Just the reverse. They fed slaves who happened to displease them to the morays."

"Ohhh, I wondered why I haven't seen a slave around this place."

"Fresh out," he answered. "Snowy was ravenous this morning. So I guess I'll have to make your drinks myself. What'll it be?"

"Vodka and tonic sounds good."

"Scotch and water," Meg said.

"Coming right up. Make yourselves at home." He flashed another of those killer smiles and disappeared into what I assumed was the kitchen.

"I wonder what he does feed that thing," I murmured.

Meg wandered over to the couch, kicked off her sandals, and sank back against the downy soft cushions. "He's really very nice, Carrie. I don't know what your problem is."

"Aside from the fact that he has a slave-eating eel for a pet, I've got no problem," I replied, sitting beside her and propping my aching foot up on the coffee table. "Wanna bet he's got a gator in the basement?"

"They don't have basements in Key West. Can't dig that deep. Too much coral."

"Well, let's stay out of his bedroom."

She looked at me, faintly amused. "The thought of going into his bedroom hadn't crossed my mind. Maybe you're attracted to him and don't know how to deal with it."

"Oh, please."

"He is damned attractive, isn't he?"

"You'd have to be catatonic not to think so. But he's not my—"

"It wouldn't be the worst thing for you to start dating now that you and Ted are taking a breather. Might make you appreciate what you have."

"Something tells me Jonathan and I don't have a helluva lot in common."

"Well, try giving him a break. He's been a real help to me."

"How much do you know about him? Did he ever mention he's a marine biologist, for instance?"

"It never came up. I know he's a diver. And I know he tried to help Pete."

"Do you?"

She was annoyed. "What're you trying to say?"

Meg is probably the closest I'll ever come to having a sister, and I didn't want to upset her more than she was already. Still, she was vulnerable now and not thinking as practically as she might. I chose my words carefully. "Just that you only know what he told you. There wasn't anyone else there."

It took a few seconds for my meaning to penetrate. When it did she sat straight up and grabbed my wrist. "What are you insinuating?" she whispered. "That you think he was involved in what happened?"

I cast a nervous peek over my shoulder at the door. "I don't know," I hissed back. "I just wonder why he always seems to be around."

"How about I make you guys dinner tonight?" Jonathan's voice resounded loudly from the doorway, sending the fish scurrying. I caught my breath, wondering what he might have heard, and guiltily removed my foot from the table.

"We have plans," Meg said coolly. "Can we take a rain check?"

"Sure." He put the tray with the drinks and a dish of chips down on the glass coffee table. "Where're you off to?"

"Someone Carrie met on the plane invited us out for dinner," Meg said. "He has some idea about getting some friends to . . . um . . ." She stopped, catching herself.

". . . to join us, help get Meg's mind off things," I chimed in, hoping he hadn't noticed the break. "But Meg isn't feeling up to a lot of company, so she's not sure she wants to come."

"Be good for you to get out," he said to Meg, sounding sincere. "Where're you going?"

Meg reached for her drink. "Carrie made the plans."

"I forget the name of the place." I took a sip of the refreshing tonic. "I have it written down by Meg's phone." Reaching for a handful of chips, I stuffed them into my mouth, precluding further inquiries.

Meg concentrated on polishing off her drink and said little during the rest of the time we were there. Jonathan went on with his mini-lecture on the habits and feeding of marine life. I kept my eyes on his face, which despite my reservations about him was infinitely nicer to look at than the gyrating, sloshing wall. Intermittently, I asked a few semiintelligent questions. We all avoided the subject that was uppermost in our thoughts. I know why I did. Jonathan, I assume, to give him credit, was trying to distract Meg, keep her from dwelling on her troubles.

By five o'clock Meg and I were back at Mrs. Larrabee's B&B.

FIRST THING I DID after kicking off my shoes was find a big towel, empty four trays of ice cubes into it, and put my leg up on the couch with the ice pack nestled firmly under a cushion to keep it in place. Emotionally spent, Meg had gone to lie down in the bedroom. I waited an hour and then I called Park City. I'd put it off for as long as I reasonably could, but I knew the children would be worried at not hearing from me. I was going to have to tell them where I was and what had happened.

Even allowing for the time difference, I figured the lifts would have closed and the kids would be back at the condo. I was right. Allie answered the phone.

"Hi, sweetheart."

"Mom? Where've you been? Why haven't you called us?"

Funny how the tables turn as your children get older, and you find yourself having to explain your whereabouts to them. "I did, honey, yesterday, but I got the answering machine and didn't leave a message. How are you? Having a great time?"

"Yeah, snow's outrageous. Fantastic cover. No blue ice at all."

"Sounds wonderful. I'm green with envy."

"I called the house last night real late to wish you Merry Christmas, and you weren't home. Didn't you get my message?" Her tone was accusatory.

"I'm not home, Allie."

"Where are you?"

"I'm in Key West with Meg."

"When did you decide to do that? Why didn't you tell us you were going?"

I could hear Matt's voice in the background. "Where is she? Tell her I won a bronze in the Nastar. Tell her—"

"Shut up, Matt! Mom, how come you decided—"

"Where's Dad, Allie? Is he there with you?" My children were close with Meg. I didn't want them hearing this news without an adult present.

"He and Suzanne went to a cocktail party."

The one time I really want him with the kids and he's unavailable. I took a deep breath. "Allie, Meg's had a . . . something happened to Pete and Kev during a practice run. I came down here to be with her."

There was dread in Allie's voice. "What do you mean? Are they okay?"

My children have had their nice, safe suburban childhood shattered, not just by Rich's and my divorce, but by the murders of two people who they knew. They weren't attached to Rich's girlfriends, but they knew them. Being acquainted with an actual murder victim is traumatic enough for an adult; it can leave lasting scars on children. They both see a therapist, but there are effects that may take years to erase. I was going to have to tell them what had happened to Kev and Pete, but very carefully. I didn't have to tell them what the police suspected. No way was I going to mention the M word.

"We're not sure what's happened to Kev, honey, but we think he may have made it to shore. The police haven't found him yet, though."

That didn't sound too bad.

"What . . . what happened to Pete?"

There was no way around it. "Pete . . . didn't make it."

"Oh, Mom. Oh, Mom! God! Poor Meg. God! She must be like . . . totally freaked!"

Matt's voice. "What happened? What happened? Allie, gimme the phone. Lemme speak to Mom."

There was a pulling match and then Matt's voice came on the line. "Mom?"

"Hi, love."

"Mom, what happened? Why're you in Key West?"

I went through it again. Yes, Ted knew about it. He was being very helpful, taking care of Horty. Yes, it was very nice of him. "I'm going to stay for the funeral, but I'll be home by the time vacation's over and you get back," I said.

"Mom?" Matt's voice, tremulous.

"What, sweetheart?"

"Tell Meg . . . tell Meg to . . . tell her I . . . I just know Kev's okay. I'll ask God to make him okay."

My sweet Mattie, who wasn't always on the best of terms with his religious-school teachers, probably had a better relationship with God than any of us. I swallowed. "You do that, honey."

"I will. Bye."

"I love you, Matt."

"Me too. Here's Allie."

"You want me to fly down and help, Mom? I'm pretty sure I could get Daddy to pay my fare."

I was taken aback by the sudden maturity in her voice, by the offer to give up her vacation. Both my children, coming through when it counted.

"Thanks, sweetheart, but I need you to watch out for Mattie for me."

"Okay." She didn't say anything for a minute. I wished I could put my arms around her, assure her everything was going to be all right.

"Give Meg my love, Mom," she managed finally. "Tell her I—" Her voice caught.

"I'll tell her you're pulling for Kev, honey." I gave her Meg's phone number, told her they should try very hard not to let all this spoil their vacation. When I hung up I was as exhausted as if I'd run a marathon. I followed Meg's example and curled up on the couch. I had a good hour before I'd have to leave for dinner with Simon Banion. I closed my eyes and drifted off.

I AM RUNNING ALONGSIDE THE *pier. It is foggy and cold, and the wind and mist are whipping my face. I look out over the tormented sea and see a white boat with silver and black stripes and a gigantic diamond painted across the hull. And Meg and Kev are on the deck and she is clutching him to her, but the wind is tearing him from her grasp and he is sucked over the side. She screams a name, but it is Pete's name and it is Pete in the water and I watch helplessly as a huge spotted moray eel rises out of the water, opens its mouth, and swallows him whole. . . . And then I am in the water and the eel is coming for me. And my feet feel heavy. . . . I cannot swim, I cannot kick . . .*

MAKING A GARGANTUAN EFFORT, I kicked. The ice pack and cushion went flying and I sat up, shivering, damp from head to foot as though I'd actually been in water. My clothes were sticking to me, my hair felt plastered to my head, and the air-conditioning chilled my body. Wide awake, I glanced at my watch. Nearly seven o'clock. I reached for my robe, peeled my clothes off, and wrapped myself in the warm, dry terry cloth.

The bathroom was off Meg's bedroom, and I knocked gently at her door. "Meg?"

"Come on in."

Her eyes were wide open, but she didn't sit up when I tiptoed in. I limped over and perched on the edge of her bed.

"You up to coming tonight?" I asked.

"Not really. You mind going alone?"

"I guess not. Is it all right with you if I give Banion the okay to get his friends going on a search? I don't want to give permission if you have any objections."

She turned her face to the wall. "I don't care, Carrie. Do what you want."

I got up. "I won't be late. I promise."

"You'd better not try walking on that ankle. Call a cab."

A half hour later, showered and dressed in my favorite ankle-length summer cotton dress—which at least partially hid the Ace—I got out of the taxi on a tiny narrow side street and walked down a tree-lined alleyway into the courtyard of Christopher House.

If I ever have a mad, passionate love affair, which doesn't seem too likely at the moment, Christopher House is where I want to have it. The plant-splashed courtyard was tucked behind a little painted cottage so that it couldn't be seen from the street. In the center of the yard, an old mahogany tree presided over scattered lounge chairs and tables, while off to the side, ringing a small kidney-shaped swimming pool, traveler palms and coconut palms provided shade. The scent of what seemed like hundreds of tropical flowers sweetened the air.

It was dusk by the time the taxi dropped me off, and the courtyard was empty except for a pool boy who was busily engaged in folding up lounge chairs. I gave him a smile and a nod and inquired where the restaurant was. He directed me to a lobby dominated by a wood staircase with gingerbready carved posts in the shape of pineapples. Huge urns filled with royal poinciana and bougainvillea stood on either side of the entranceway, and a delicate candelabra chandelier hung over a flower-bordered oval rug. I could see the terrace restaurant just beyond the registration desk. Now that I was actually here, I couldn't figure out a way to get the information I wanted. I picked up several brochures displayed on a rack near the desk, studied them intently as though I were a tourist. Finally, I approached the desk clerk.

"Excuse me . . ."

"Can I help you?" She was young and pretty, in her early twenties—like eighty percent of the Key West population. Her blond hair was long and straight, she had a pert, upturned nose, and was wearing white shorts and a blue shirt with the hotel's logo on the pocket. The writing above the pocket said *My name is Debby. I'm here to help.* That would, I hoped, prove to be true.

"Yes, uh . . . Debby," I said in my friendliest manner. "I'm meeting some people here for dinner—"

"Oh, you want the terrace. It's just there to the right."

"Yes, I know. But I'm a little early and I thought I'd inquire about, uh . . . a reservation for New Year's Eve."

"Oh, I'm sorry, we're all booked for New Year's," she said. "Every place around here is."

"I thought you would be, so what I'd like to do is see if I could join some friends. Just for the festivities, I mean. I already have a place to stay."

She looked doubtful, but pulled out the reservation book. "Gee, I don't know. New Year's Eve the tables're usually set pretty close together. Hard to squeeze extras in. What's the name?"

Would the reservation be under Kevin's name? I hadn't a clue.

"Try Reilly."

She studied the book, shook her head. "No Reilly. Maybe it's under somebody else's name?"

"It could be. May I see the book? I might recognize someone."

I could see her hesitation, took a stab. "Peters. I think they're with the Peters. Could you try that?"

Her eyes slid down the page. "Oh, yes, here it is. K. Peters. Would that be them?"

My throat tightened, rendering me momentarily unable to answer.

"It's a party of—excuse me a minute." She reached for the phone, which was ringing insistently. "Reservations."

I tried reading upside down. Not a skill I'd ever needed to develop. No luck. Debby went on with her conversation, her attention shifting between her notepad and the tall, dark-haired, muscular young man who'd just walked through the entrance. I took advantage of the situation, leaned my elbows on the counter, and accidentally shoved the book sideways. Twisting my neck, I ran my eyes down the list. There it was. *K. Peters. Party of four.* K. Could that be for Kevin? Did that mean he was alive and had made this reservation using the two first names? Maybe someone else had made the reservation. Maybe there was a real K. Peters. Somehow I was going to have to get here on New Year's Eve. Furtively, I scanned the rest of the list. At the bottom a name jumped out at me. *Jonathan Olsen. Party of two.*

Clearly Jonathan was as determined as I to find out who was going to show up on New Year's Eve. Why was he so interested? How had he managed to get a reservation at the last minute? I glanced over at Debby, pictured Jonathan smiling down at her, a lock of white-blond hair falling over his forehead as he released those powerful pheromones. Debby would've been Play-Doh in his ruggedly callused hands. Thirty seconds—*zap*—and little Debby would've agreed to wait on the table herself. But who was the other person in his party of two? Certainly he wasn't thinking of asking Meg. Or me. Maybe his having a New Year's Eve reservation here was a coincidence. Maybe he'd made it much earlier. No, if that were so, wouldn't he have mentioned it when he told me about the call?

"Sorry." Debby returned her attention to me. "Where was I? Oh, yes, K. Peters. It's a party of four, and our tables seating four really don't have room for anyone else. If it'd been a larger party, we might've been able to—"

"It doesn't matter," I interjected when she paused for breath. "It's the wrong Peters. My friend's name is . . . uh, Ted. For Theodore," I added unnecessarily. Only half a lie. I did have a friend named Ted for Theodore.

"Oh," she said. "Well, sorry I couldn't help you. Hope you find someplace else to go." She turned a brilliant smile on Tall, Dark, and Sexy, who by now was standing beside me.

My "thanks anyway" fell on deaf ears. I limped over to a little alcove and sank into a chair, trying to recall what Jonathan had said the exact message from the woman on the phone had been. *It was set for New Year's Eve at Christopher House.* That was it. But was Jonathan telling me the whole truth, everything the woman had said? He'd intimated that if Kev was alive he was deliberately not contacting Meg because he had some other agenda.

I forced my thoughts back to my reasons for being here. The hands on my watch read eight-twenty. I glanced around the lobby, noticed a short, stocky woman in a flowered dress and walking shoes coming up on a gray-haired man wearing a rumpled light-gray sport jacket. I started to get to my feet, certain this must be Banion and his friend, but when the man turned I realized he was older than my airplane companion. I concluded we'd missed each other and they were already in the dining room, so I grabbed my handbag and headed for the terrace.

He saw me just as I saw him, waved, and beckoned me to a table by a window in the back corner. I made my halting way through the crowded, noisy restaurant, hesitating briefly as my eyes lit on his companion. Surely this wasn't Mr. Banion's girlfriend, the woman who was so afraid of flying. This woman was several years younger than I and didn't look as though she were afraid of anything.

"Ms. Carlin—Caroline," he greeted me. "May I call you Caroline?"

The last person to call me Caroline was my fifth-grade teacher. "Carrie," I responded, and almost tripped over his umbrella propped against my chair.

"I'm so sorry," he said, removing the umbrella and reaching out an arm to steady me. "Let me take that. Please, sit down. I'd like you to meet my friend, Francine."

I held out my hand to the cool, strikingly beautiful brunette sitting opposite me. "Hi. Nice to meet you."

"Nice to meet you too."

Her voice was pleasant, with a slightly sexy hoarseness. "You must forgive Simon. He drags that umbrella everywhere. Like the British, he believes in being prepared." The manicured hand that reached out to clasp mine showcased an emerald and diamond ring and several gold bracelets. Her green silk pants outfit was simple and elegant—Ungaro or Valentino or some other outrageously expensive Italian designer with a surname ending in O. Self-consciously, I smoothed the skirt of my twice-marked-down Liz Claiborne.

"Where is Mrs. Reilly?" Simon asked.

"I'm sorry, she didn't feel up to coming."

He glanced at Francine, then back at me. "I am sorry. We would have liked to compliment her on her work. She's a talented woman."

"I'll tell her you said so. She did ask me to thank you for your offer. She'd appreciate whatever you can do to help."

"We'll get to that later. Would you care for a drink?"

I noticed a bottle of Puligny Montrachet—one of my favorites in my more affluent days—nestled in a bucket of ice. "White wine would be fine."

The waiter hovered, poised to fulfill our every need. I ordered something exotic with crab and seaweed that tasted ambrosial, and the light, crisp wine flowed like beer at a fraternity party. Money, it seemed, was not one of Banion's problems. It was one of mine, and I'd refused an appetizer, aware of how quickly the bill could run up in a place like this.

Francine kept up a steady stream of conversation about a recent trip to Australia and about the history of Key West and the sights I absolutely should not miss while here. She gave no indication that she regarded this evening as anything other than a pleasant social occasion. I did my best to listen to her chatter, but my attention kept shifting to Simon, waiting for him to say something about the search.

"So you're a cat person," Francine commented out of the blue as the waiter cleared away the main course.

We were going to talk about *cats?* "Uh . . . yes. How'd you know?" I asked.

"Sy mentioned it."

I couldn't recall discussing my cats with Simon on the plane. "I like animals in general," I replied, polite to the end. "So do my children. We have three cats and a dog."

"The cats are Siamese, aren't they?" Simon chimed in. "Named after some opera singers?"

"Luciano, Placido, and José." I must've been dead drunk on that plane. For the life of me I couldn't remember telling him that.

"Cute," Francine drawled. "Well, you really must see Hemingway House. The place is full of history. He had fifty, you know. Cats, I mean. There are about forty still living on the premises, all descendants of the ones Hemingway kept, they say. They're fed and cared for by the grounds keepers."

"Really," I murmured, wishing her on Hemingway's premises now so Simon and I could get down to business.

Over key lime pie that he insisted on ordering for me, Francine asked what had happened to my ankle. I said I'd tripped over a boat trailer, and Simon "tut-tutted" solicitously. After my second cup of coffee, when I'd just about decided Meg had been right about Banion, Francine rose and excused herself, pleading an early-morning sailing lesson.

"I believe you and Sy have a lot to discuss," she said, displaying perfect white teeth, "so I'll just take myself off. Maybe you'll join us for the races. We have a wonderful view from the Havana Docks Bar at the Pier House."

"Thanks, but I don't think so. I doubt I'll be watching the races."

"Oh, you never know," she said enigmatically. "You might change your mind." And blowing a kiss to Simon, she breezed off.

Banion's manner was beginning to strike me as bizarre. The wine was going to my head and I refused his offer of an after-dinner drink, afraid I'd say something to that effect. I considered offering to pay my share of the bill, then decided I wouldn't. He'd invited me to dinner, and it was looking more and more likely that he'd gotten me here under false pretenses. A little of my annoyance found its way to my tongue. "I can't help wondering how Francine could think I'd have any desire to see a boat race after—"

"Probably," he interrupted, signaling the waiter for the check, "because she's aware there's an excellent chance your friend's husband is alive."

When he turned back to me, the retiring little man I'd met on the airplane had vanished, replaced by a self-assured, younger-seeming, very much in-charge man of the world. "That being the case," he went on, "I assume she was thinking there's a good possibility he'll show up at the races and that you and your friend, Meg, would want to be there."

I was speechless, which hardly ever happens to me. Then I got angry. "What's this about? Who are you?"

"Please don't be upset," he said soothingly. "We had to be certain you could be trusted."

"We?" I snapped. "You mean you and your *friend*?" That was uncalled for, but I don't like being deceived, and anyway, I have this thing about May–December relationships.

He ignored the remark and, reaching into his jacket pocket, pulled out a small black case. Shielding it from nearby inquisitive eyes, he flipped it open and spoke softly. "FBI."

I stared at the badge and the laminated card, torn between disbelief and a wild urge to laugh. "You're FBI? Come on. This is some kind of joke."

"I promise you it's no joke." He started to return the case to his pocket.

It's not difficult to get a phony ID in Florida—probably not anywhere else either if you know the right people. The guy was obviously a thrill seeker, as Meg had said. Or worse. Crazy. Maybe even dangerous. "May I see your credentials again, please?" I asked as coolly as I could manage, though I'm damned if I'd know the difference between real ones and fake ones.

He lit a cigarette and handed the case back to me. I opened it and studied the ID inside carefully. It said FBI and had an official-looking seal and a four-digit number. The photograph looked okay, but what did I know?

"I have a cell phone with me. If it would make you feel better, you can call information and ask for Miami FBI headquarters, Director Crenshaw. He'll verify who I am."

I wasn't sure what would make me feel better at this particular moment. I handed the case back, decided to play along, see what the guy had in mind. "I intend to do that. Meanwhile, I'd like your explanation."

"Sure you won't have an after-dinner drink? Brandy, or Southern Comfort, perhaps?"

"I don't want anything but an explanation."

He took a drag, his eyes carefully sweeping the surrounding tables, doing a great imitation of 007. Then he leaned forward, his manner casual, as though we were still talking about Hemingway's cats. "I've just been assigned," he said lowering his voice, "to investigate Peter Reilly's death and to find his brother. My superiors don't believe that Kevin Reilly is floating in the water somewhere. They're pretty certain he's alive and in hiding."

I leaned forward conspiratorially and whispered, "Hiding from whom?"

"From the mob. Peter Reilly's death was a mob hit.

The bureau's had a man, Special Agent Kellerman, down here working on the case for weeks."

The afternoon's events at the pier crashed in on me. Stu Kellerman, the guy in the boat with the panther on the hull who wouldn't talk to us, the guy who'd been seen drinking with Pete in Barefoot Bob's. The article on Diamantopoulos murdered over a bad business deal. My own unspoken thoughts, wondering where the money for Stargazer had come from. And the book lady's comment, hammering in my head: *"Ya don't cross the mob. Not if you want to go on breathin'."*

Could it be this guy was for real?

I looked up at the waiter, who had materialized by the table, check in hand. "I'd like an after-dinner drink, please."

"Certainly, ma'am. What can I bring you?"

I'd never tasted it, but the name seemed appropriate to the situation. "Southern Comfort," I said. "Double. Straight up. In a snifter."

"T HE POLICE THINK KEV killed Pete," I said as the strong, sweetish liquid burned its way down my esophagus into my acid stomach. Fighting fire with fire.

"We believe both men were meant to die when Peter lost control of the boat."

"I know Meg's convinced Kev's alive," I said, still not completely trusting him. He couldn't, after all, know about the phone calls. "That's wishful thinking on her part. Why do *you* think he is?"

"No body."

"I'm told it can take days, sometimes longer for a body to wash up on shore."

"Let's just say we're interested in why the mob has its soldiers out looking for him. It's important we find him before they or the police do."

"Why the police? Don't you work with the police?"

He took his time answering, half-smiled as he flicked an ash into the ashtray. "Sometimes it's better for all concerned if we function separately."

The reply made me wary. I didn't think Ted would be thrilled with it either. "Why's that? If the cops find him, they'll protect him, even if they think he's guilty."

"They'll try. They won't succeed."

I was involved with a cop. I didn't like hearing that. He saw the expressions flash across my face.

"Drugs are big business in this part of the country," he said quietly. "The temptation is great. Occasionally, a cop turns dirty."

I thought about Hanover and gulped another mouthful of Southern Comfort. It failed to comfort me. I wondered how much this guy knew. "How did Pete die?"

"Poison. Something long-acting."

"How did they . . . how do you know?"

"I can't tell you that."

"I thought the Mafia always shoots its victims in the head."

He smiled. "It's not a hard-and-fast rule."

"So where do I come in?"

He snuffed out his cigarette and, reaching across the table, took the hand that wasn't holding the glass. "You must convince your friend to give up the search. Both you and she place yourselves in danger every time you start asking questions. I have men trying to protect her, but they can't be available on a twenty-four-hour basis, and their job gets more difficult when the two of you go gallivanting all over town." His pale eyes flashed to my bandaged foot. "You were damned lucky today to have gotten away with just a sprained ankle."

I nearly dropped the snifter. "Are you saying . . . someone deliberately tried to run me down this afternoon?"

"Not you. You just got in the way. Anyway, it was only a warning. If they'd wanted to kill your friend, they'd have done it."

Kill Meg? Someone might want to kill Meg? I polished off the rest of my drink, tried to speak calmly. "Then why do you want us at the races? Won't Meg be in danger there?"

"So long as she's with me, she'll be safe."

"But what's the point? Why take a chance?"

He released my hand. "Because we think her husband will show up. He won't be able to resist. He'll probably be in disguise and he'll stay out of sight. But if he sees his wife, we believe he'll find a way to contact her. We believe he has information that could help us put a lot of people behind bars. Once we get to him, we can take steps to safeguard them both."

"He hasn't been in touch with Meg till now. If he's alive I can't believe he'd let her go on not knowing if—"

"We're not the only ones watching. He's not taking any chances with his wife's life. He's a good man."

"I know that." I mulled over everything he'd said, trying to match up, as Ted would, the disparate puzzle pieces. Something didn't fit. "I still don't understand why Pete was killed. If he owed money, he can't pay it back if he's dead."

"Oh, it's much more complicated than that." Banion

pushed back his chair, picked up the umbrella, and got to his feet. "Can you walk for a bit on that ankle?"

I rose, a little unsteadily after the last drink. "I'm fine. I planned to try and walk home."

"I'd prefer you didn't. I'll put you in a cab."

"That's not necessary. Really. It's not far. I can—"

"I'd like to make certain you get where you're going."

"Oh." I glanced around nervously. "Okay."

We didn't talk till we hit Duval Street. I felt better once we'd passed through the small alleyway and were out among the crowds on the main thoroughfare. It had begun to drizzle, the misty rain so light I hardly felt it on my bare arms.

Banion spoke in a flat voice. "This is how we've pieced it together. Through a mutual friend, Peter Reilly met some people who offered him the stake he needed to get his boat business going."

"Who was that?"

"I'm not at liberty to say. But I will tell you we have him under surveillance."

Suddenly the sky opened up and we found cover under the awning of a bathing-suit shop. Inside of twenty seconds we were surrounded by a group of young people, like us seeking to escape a drenching. They jostled against us as they admired the bikinied mannequins in the window. Banion pulled me close and spoke into my ear.

"I'm not sure if Reilly knew who they were initially," he said. "Certainly he wasn't equipped to swim in such shark-infested waters. It wasn't long before he was in to them for a great deal of money and unable to meet the monthly payments. They wanted favors in exchange for forgiving his timely payment of the debt."

"What kind of favors?"

"Having to do with drug-running on his boat. His brother got wind of it from someone he knew in Danbury. Kicked up a fuss, and when he got out and came to Key West, he tried to renegotiate the contract. That wasn't what the mob had in mind. It got someone high up extremely upset. Upset enough to order a different kind of contract."

You don't cross the mob, sang in my head.

"The situation isn't out of control yet. With your cooperation we can bring Kevin Reilly in."

"But you can't hide him forever! They'll find him. I've read—"

"That's a bridge to be crossed when we're there." He hailed a passing cab, which ignored him. "Meantime, the less anyone knows, the better chance we have of getting to him before they do."

"I'm not about to broadcast this to the media," I said shakily.

Two other cabs, one pink and one yellow, passed us by, filled with people. Banion gripped my arm, and there was urgency in his voice. "I mean no one, absolutely no one, can know who I am. That includes your friend and your boyfriend."

I was stunned. "You don't want me to tell Meg? What if she'd come with me tonight?"

"That's why Francine was there. She'd have found some excuse to take her for a walk in the garden or asked her to pin something up in the ladies' room. Your sprained ankle would have kept you in your chair."

"But how do you expect me to persuade her to stop looking for Kev? Or to go to the races, for that matter? She'll never agree—"

"We're relying on you to come up with a convincing reason."

The FBI was relying on me.

A taxi pulled up to the curb, and Banion, swifter than I would've thought him capable, beat the crowd of teenagers. Opening the door, he handed me in, gave the driver my address, and pressed a bill into his hand and a card into mine. "In an emergency you can reach me at this number," he whispered in my ear. "Remember, no one must know about me. If my cover gets blown, you're out in the cold."

The door slammed shut and he waved the driver on. From the window of the taxi, through a veil of shimmering raindrops, I watched him metamorphose back into the pleasant, mild-mannered little man of American Airlines Flight 967.

"I'm counting on you," he mouthed. Then, opening his umbrella, he shuffled off down the street.

As I LIMPED UP the steps to Meg's suite of rooms, my mind was in chaos, a jumble of force-fed facts that I kept wanting to push away. Everything Banion had told me sounded to my suburban, middle-class ears like a plot from a Scorsese film. I once saw an interview in which Scorsese said he drew his story lines from real life, from events remembered from his childhood. I'd considered the answer an appeal to sensationalism to attract audiences. How many people grew up in that type of environment? Nobody *I* knew was involved with criminal types—if, of course, I didn't count Ted . . . and, well, now Pete and Kev . . . and Simon Banion.

I guess I owe Mr. Scorsese an apology.

I pondered, as I searched in my bag for the key Meg

had lent me, how much of what went on at dinner I should tell her. She was bound to ask questions. I'd have to come up with some reason why there would be no private flotilla. Banion's invitation to call FBI headquarters came back to me. He'd been pretty convincing, but just to be on the safe side, I planned to check him out first thing in the morning. He'd been explicit about not wanting Meg to know his true identity, but she was my dearest friend. She deserved some respite from the unbearable anxiety. It'd be a trade-off, one set of worries for another; still, just knowing Kev was thought to be alive by the FBI was bound to be a relief. Or was it? How would it help her at this point to know Pete's death had been a mob hit? If it meant gambling with Kevin's life, would she thank me down the line? And what was I supposed to do about Ted? He has an uncanny nose for the truth, which is what makes him a good cop, and I'm a pathetic liar. I couldn't even get away with that "our emotions can't be trusted" stuff I'd tried on Christmas Eve. Ted would know in a New York minute I was holding something back.

I paused on the landing, annoyed to find that the light in the upstairs hallway had blown and Lady Larrabee hadn't gotten around to replacing it. I had to fumble in the dark in search of the keyhole, adding to the jitters I was feeling as an aftermath of my conversation with Banion.

"You're falling down on the job, Millie. I definitely will not recommend this place to *Life Styles of the Rich and Famous*," I grumbled aloud, more to hear my own voice than to attempt communication with the recalcitrant landlady. Finally locating the evasive lock, I slipped my key in, pushed the door open, and stepped into a pitch-black living room. Without the glow of the hall light, I couldn't see where the switch was. I felt around near the doorjamb, but it wasn't where it should be. Meg must have closed the curtains, because there wasn't even a sliver of moonlight. I let my handbag slide to the floor and ran my fingers up and down the wall, cursing softly. Nothing. Then I remembered the lamp table next to the Christmas tree. I groped my way across the room like a blind woman, bumped into a chair, banged into the tree, and heard some ornaments crash. "Chrissake, Carrie," I muttered under my breath, "making enough noise to wake the dead."

My hands came in contact with smooth wood. I reached up and touched the grainy fabric of the lamp-shade, found the chain, pulled it, and, hallelujah, there was light! Dismayed, I took in the shattered remains of several of Meg's delicate nautical ornaments at my feet. I bent to pick up the pieces—and froze. Mildred Larra-bee's mooselike form lay sprawled across the threshold between the living room and the kitchenette. No amount of noise that I might make was ever going to wake her. This was only my second corpse, but I know what classic dead looks like. Her eyes were open, the pupils fixed and dilated, and one leg was twisted under her like a broken doll. But what clinched it was the curved knife the size of Excalibur sticking out of her blood-soaked chartreuse blouse.

"This can't be happening again, this can't be happen-ing again," I heard someone saying. Then I realized it was me. The ornaments dropped from my fingers, and I was crouched over backing away when I bumped into the lamp table. I think I was swaying, but I couldn't seem to fall down. I wanted to fall down. I wanted to black out like I did the last time I discovered a dead body, but it appeared I wasn't going to be lucky twice. Blessed oblivion did not enfold me in its comforting arms. Except for my shaking knees, I remained paralyzed. Nausea rose like mercury in a thermometer on a hot day. I was well on my way to losing that expensive dinner.

Then, as suddenly as it had come, the nausea receded, and through the haze that had briefly anethetized my mind, my brain began sending messages. *Someone's killed Millie Larrabee in Meg's apartment! Get out! Get out! They might still be here!* I started moving toward the door.

"If they'd wanted to kill your friend, they'd have done it." Like the voice of Hamlet's father's ghost, Banion's words came to me. *Meg!* Where was Meg? I opened my mouth and cried her name. My legs, of their own volition, changed direction and propelled me into the bedroom.

I flipped on the light switch. There was a red splotch on the pillow.

"Oh, God! Meg!" I screamed. "Oh, God, oh God, please, please, Meg, be alive!"

"What? What's the matter?" came a groggy voice from the floor on the other side of the bed. "Christ almighty, stop yelling. My head's killing me."

A fireball of red-gold hair, matted with blood, appeared at mattress level. Meg's hands clutched her head as she struggled to a sitting position. Confusion and anger jockeyed for dominance on her face. "My head," she moaned, and stared in puzzlement at the hand that came away bloody.

My feeling of relief was so intense that it was like a rush of oxygen to an asthmatic. Sprained ankle forgotten, I sprinted around the bed and was helping her to her feet before she could push herself up. Her legs buckled, and the blood rushed from her face. As she fell back I eased her onto the bed and held her close while tears streamed unchecked down my cheeks. Seconds later her gasp startled me into looking up.

What my terror and shock had prevented me from noticing before hit me now. Drawers were open, their contents strewn everywhere. Clothes torn from hangers were left lying in heaps on the floor. Meg's handbag and camera case were upside down. Feathers from her sliced mattress and pillow floated in the air. Suitcases had been pulled from closets, their tops and insides slashed into strips. Books and papers were randomly scattered, and the curtains had been pulled off the windows and were hanging awry like half-dressed mannequins.

"What's all this?" Meg murmured in amazement.

I looked at her, stunned. "Don't you know?"

"Wait . . ." There was silence as she attempted to jog her memory. "I think I . . . it's coming back . . . Mrs. Larrabee. Mrs. Larrabee knocked on the door, said there was a different detective here to see me. She was pissed off about being disturbed so late."

I'd forgotten Millie! "Meg," I started, then stopped, not certain she could stand to see the scene in the living room.

"I was in bed. . . ." Bit by bit she began reconstructing the events. "She let herself and him in while I was putting on my robe. I don't know why, but I thought it was Ted." Gingerly, she touched the back of her head. "He hit me."

"Ted?" I exclaimed, horrified.

"No, no, it wasn't him. God, my head's killing me."

"Let me get a cold washcloth."

From the bathroom I heard her talking out loud,

trying to piece together the wisps that had begun filtering back.

"They were arguing in the other room, so I knew it wasn't Ted. And it wasn't Springer or Hanover either. I didn't recognize the voice. And then . . . and then I . . ."

As I rushed back into the bedroom and pressed the cold cloth to her forehead, I saw the horror registering on her face.

"Don't try to talk yet."

"I remember what happened! She shouted something, and then I heard . . . like a groan, and something fell, and there was a crash, and then I started to go for the phone on the night table, but somebody ran in here and that's when—" Her eyes flew to my face. "Carrie, where's Mrs. Larrabee?"

My expression gave it away.

"Oh, Christ, no, she can't be . . . She isn't . . ."

Miserably, I nodded.

A whisper. "Where?"

"In the living room. But I don't think you should . . . you shouldn't go in there yet. You've had a shock and you're hurt. We'll call the police and—"

I couldn't stop her. She struggled to her feet, and all I could do was follow, because when Meg makes up her mind, there's no changing it. "There might be prints," I, the homicide expert, called after her. "Don't touch the knife."

When I got to the doorway, she had stopped several feet from the body. Her own body had gone rigid, and her voice drifted back to me, barely audible over the whir of the air conditioner. "That's not a knife." And then she was keening. "It's a machete. Oh, my God, Carrie, it's a machete!"

11

ARE YOU CERTAIN THAT wasn't your husband who came in with the landlady?"

We were in the downstairs sitting room: Meg—still in her robe, head patched with a bandage hastily applied by a shocked-speechless paramedic—me, and the ever-churlish Detective Hanover. Meg answered him through clenched teeth.

"I know my husband's voice. Besides which, the man hit me. You think my husband would have attacked me?"

"Depends how he wanted it to look. If his intention was to throw suspicion off himself . . . or you . . ."

Leaning casually against the doorjamb, Hanover looked like he was on his way to a day at the beach. He was wearing chinos and a T-shirt, which displayed a huge yellow and purple shark with a formidable set of choppers in hot pursuit of a school of terrified bluefish. The letters splashed across his chest said *Sun Lover*, but the expression on his face mirrored the shark's. If I'd had a machete in my hand, his head would've rolled.

Garson Springer was upstairs in Meg's rooms directing a cadre of professionals, who were, I supposed, engaged in dusting for fingerprints, snapping photographs, etc., procedures with which I was, unfortunately, familiar. Thus we were left to be interrogated by Detective Jaws.

Everything about the man infuriated me—his inappropriate attire, his manner, and at the moment especially the direction in which he was leading the conversation.

I put my arm around Meg, more to keep her upright than to comfort her. Her face looked as washed out as an overbleached hospital sheet. I wasn't sure how much blood she'd lost, but Hanover's badgering had drained whatever flush had remained in her cheeks after the sight of the unfortunate Mrs. L.

"I thought you'd concluded Kevin Reilly was probably dead," I snapped. "Now you're insinuating that, without any motive that makes sense, he committed a double murder and bludgeoned his wife in the bargain."

"I'm insinuating nothing. I'm hypothesizing."

"Well, why don't you hypothesize something that might actually have a chance of leading somewhere? Like trying to figure out what this guy was looking for."

"You tell me." He looked straight at Meg.

"I don't know."

"By the state of those rooms, he certainly was looking for something. And whatever it was he wanted it bad enough to kill for it."

What *bad* the killer been looking for? I went over in my mind the condition of the room. Why had the mattress and the pillows been slashed? In a couple of places floorboards had been torn up. Money was the obvious conclusion. Did they believe Kev had stashed cash somewhere in the apartment? If Pete had owed money to the mob and they believed he'd had it in his possession but hadn't been making his payments to them, then they would come after it. Had they found it? I studied Meg's face. Did she know something she wasn't telling me? Would she tell me if I asked?

"You and your husband keep cash in the apartment?" Hanover asked.

"Grocery money."

"How about your brother-in-law?"

"He had a separate room. You know that. You've impounded his belongings."

"Have you checked to see if anything's missing?"

Meg shook her head. "I never went back in the bedroom after we called you."

"We didn't want to touch anything," I put in, hoping to make points with the guy. "You know, disturb the crime scene."

"I can see you're familiar with police procedure."

That'll teach me to brown-nose.

Hanover sauntered across the room and pulled up a chair, sitting so unpleasantly close to us I could smell his after-shave. I thought about Banion's inference about dirty cops. If I had to choose a candidate, he'd top the list.

"I find it odd that the perpetrator would have stabbed the Larrabee woman, but only knocked Mrs. Reilly unconscious. I don't suppose it was because he ran out of machetes. I wonder if you might have a theory about that?"

Meg leaned back against the headrest on the pastel wicker love seat and closed her eyes. When she spoke, her voice was as drained of emotion as her face was of color. "Detective Hanover, I have a hideous headache. I have no theories or explanations for anything that's happened. I don't know the answers to any of your questions. I only know that the man who was in the living room tonight definitely wasn't my husband. You can believe my story or not, but no matter how many times you ask me to repeat it, I'll tell you the same thing. Because it's the truth and it's the only story I've got."

Strangely enough, I thought he did believe her, because he shifted position, focusing his unwanted attentions on me.

"Where were you this evening?"

Uh-oh. Sticky. "I had dinner with someone I met on the plane coming down here."

"Male or female?" he inquired with exaggerated politeness.

My fists clenched, but I answered politely. "It was a couple."

He fished a dog-eared notebook out of his pocket. "Name?"

There was no way out of it. "Banion."

"Tourists?"

"I assume they're here for the races."

"Where did you have dinner?"

Damn! "Christopher House." The name, however, apparently meant nothing to him.

"Where are these people staying?"

"I . . . don't know."

"You don't know? You generally pick up strangers on airplanes, have dinner with them, and don't even inquire where they're staying?"

Sy Banion was definitely not going to like this. "They . . . might be staying at Pier House. At least, they invited us to watch the races with them there." I didn't know Francine's last name, and fortunately, Hanover assumed the couple I'd had dinner with were married.

He scrawled something, returned the notebook to his pocket, leaned back in the chair till it tottered on two legs while he scratched his nose, and stared at a moth that was relentlessly beating its wings against a light fixture on the wall. "Ms. Carlin," he drawled, his eyes trained on the suicidal moth. "You seem to have a penchant for finding bodies."

The words were almost the same words Ted had spoken to me when I found the other body. I know Ted didn't tell him about that. He must've pulled it up on microfiche from some old newspaper. One of the disadvantages of today's technology. There's not a thing that's ever happened to any of us that isn't recorded somewhere.

"Look," I said, empathizing with the moth. "I'm staying here in this B&B with my friend. I went out for a nice dinner, came back, walked in, and saw the woman dead on the floor. I didn't kill her. And whatever you may think, I don't go looking for this sort of thing. I'm a biofeedback person, for God's sake!"

He stared at me blankly. "You're a what?"

My voice rose to a screech. "A biofeedback person, a biofeedback person! I teach people to relax. That's how I make my living. I chose a profession that teaches you how to deal with stress. I'm trained to control my emotions!" By now I was yelling at the top of my voice. "But who the hell could stay calm in these circumstances? I almost had a heart attack. I almost lost an excellent meal. I don't think I'll ever eat again. So why don't you get the hell out of my face and go find whoever did this godawful thing? And while you're at it, find Kevin Reilly!"

I guess he finally figured I was on the verge of hysteria, because his tone became placating. "Only a few more questions."

My sigh was more like a howl, and Meg reached over and put her hand on mine.

"Who knew you weren't going to be here tonight?"

"No one."

"Except your airplane friend."

"Well, of course, except him." This cop had a serious learning disability. "But then, he wasn't out of my sight all evening. So aside from the fact that we just met, so he could have no possible motive for killing anyone I know or for searching these rooms for God knows what—"

He turned to Meg. "Can you think of anyone else who knew you would be alone here tonight?"

"No one knew," I reiterated, "because it was a last-minute decision. Meg was going to come with me. It wasn't until we got back from Jonathan's—" I stopped, because I suddenly remembered who else had known our plans this evening. I could tell by Meg's expression that the same thought had just occurred to her.

Hanover caught our exchange of glances. "Jonathan who?"

Meg frowned and wagged her head warningly, but I ignored her. Jonathan might have the face of an angel, but if there was even a remote possibility that along with fish-collecting this guy's hobbies included hitting for the mob, I sure as hell wasn't going to cover for him.

"Jonathan Olsen," I mumbled, avoiding Meg's eyes. "The diver who pulled Pete Reilly out of the bay."

BEFORE THE APARTMENT WAS sealed off, Springer instructed us to pack a few things to wear the following day and then crash in the sitting room for the rest of the night. I told Meg to stay put, a suggestion to which she readily acquiesced, and reluctantly followed Springer up the stairs and back into the apartment. I kept my eyes determinedly glued to his blue striped shirt to avoid seeing the covered form lying like an enormous sack of cement near the kitchenette. Poor Millie Larrabee. If she'd gone with her original instinct and thrown us out when she'd threatened to, she'd still be alive. I remembered my promise to "take care" of her before I left. Well, that wouldn't be necessary now. Someone had already done that.

"That could've been you," Springer said, watching me through narrowed eyes.

A shiver ran through me. He was right. Had I been sleeping in that living room as I would have been if I'd decided against meeting Banion, my children would now be . . .

"What in hell have you people gotten yourselves mixed up in?"

"I don't know. I swear."

He threw a disgusted look my way and preceded me into the bedroom. "Make it fast and don't disturb anything."

I paused in the doorway and glanced around the bedroom, averting my eyes from the bloody pillow, searching for that secret hiding place the killer had overlooked. Or maybe he hadn't overlooked it. Maybe he'd found the loot. *The loot.* In my head I'd already determined it was money the mob was after.

I jumped as Springer cleared his throat, a hint for me to move my butt, and scurried around snatching up pieces of clothing off the floor. When I'd put together enough to outfit us both for at least a couple of days, I stuffed the things that had spilled out of Meg's handbag, along with her camera and my laptop, into one of the mutilated suitcases.

"I'd like to get our toothbrushes and a few cosmetics. Is that okay?"

"Go ahead." But he followed me into the bathroom and stood watching, as though sure I'd give away the secret location.

The bathroom was as colossal a mess as the other rooms. The medicine chest and our cosmetics bags had been ransacked, but I managed to salvage a few necessities.

As we made our way downstairs, I could see that the commotion had awakened several of the guests. A couple of uniforms herded them back into their rooms with the brief explanation that there'd been an unfortunate accident and Mrs. Larrabee would be unable to provide them with their continental breakfast in the morning. Most were too disconcerted by the police presence to object, but out of the corner of my eye, I caught one guy snapping a picture as I passed by him. I had visions of my stepmother opening the morning newspaper and seeing my haggard face on the front page. I'd be barred from Worcester, Massachusetts, for life.

"I'll take care of it," Springer said brusquely when I voiced my misgivings. "There'll be an officer outside here all night." He handed me blankets and pillows he'd taken from the studio couch. "Try to get a few hours sleep."

As traumatized as I was, I was also exhausted, and the word *sleep* sounded inviting. Meg, too, despite the events of the night, was dozing on the love seat. I covered her with a blanket and crawled into the armchair, where I curled up like a question mark and gave sleeping a shot.

"We've got to find someplace else to stay," I murmured after fifteen minutes of no success.

"We'll worry about it tomorrow. I'm too wiped to think."

So was I, but try as I might, sleep wouldn't come. I tossed and turned, determined to turn off the mind chatter. I concentrated on my breathing. I relaxed muscle after muscle progressively, retreated to my "tree house," mumbled my focus word—*Caaalmmm*—thirty or forty times.

"Meg," I whispered, finally giving up.

"Mmm?"

"Is there anything, anything at all you haven't told me?"

No answer. I raised myself up and peeked over at her. Her eyes were closed. I couldn't tell if she was asleep. Maybe she was. Or maybe she just didn't want to talk.

I WAS AWAKENED AT 6:00 A.M. by a sharp knock. Bleary-eyed, I staggered to the door and opened it. A young policeman, whom I assumed was the one on guard duty all night, apologized politely in a pleasant southern twang for disturbing us so early.

"I'm Officer Fleming, ma'am," he said. "Lieutenant Springer thinks you might want to vacate the premises before the media shows up. They can be a mite . . . aggressive."

I came alert. I didn't know where Meg and I were going, but there was no question it would be unwise to stay around here and play *Meet the Press.*

"Thanks," I replied, starting to close the door. "We'll be ready in a few minutes."

"Uh . . . he also said if you find a place to stay you should call him from there. I'm to drive you wherever you want, and if you can't locate a vacancy, you're to come with me to Stock Island."

Meg was already putting on her sneakers when I turned around. She looked a little brighter than she had last night—hardly robust, but some color had returned to her cheeks.

"You need to get that bandage changed," I said as I reached for my shoes. "Let's get some breakfast, and then we'll stop by the nearest ER. We have transportation, courtesy of Key West's finest."

I'd slept fully clothed, and Meg had her jeans and T-shirt on before I was out of the rest room in the lobby. I saw the first of the camera crews arriving as we pulled away.

"Eyes and ears of the world," Fleming laughed. "Lucky they weren't camping out all night. They never sleep."

I knew that.

"Where to?"

"We need sustenance. Mind stopping at a coffee shop?"

"My pleasure, ma'am. I could go for a bite myself."

Eating places abound in Key West, and we were on Roosevelt Boulevard and pulling into Shoney's parking lot before the clock had struck seven. Meg and I found a table in a corner, while our courteous protector chose one by the window, where he could keep his eye on both the street and us. He availed himself of his "bite"— a fruit platter, sausage, bacon, three eggs, home fries, toast, and coffee. Meg and I ordered coffee and English muffins.

"We'll never get a room in this town," Meg said. "Not this week."

"How about something further out? I think I passed a Comfort Inn on the way from the airport."

"We can call the reservations hot line, but I'm sure there won't be anything. The races are a huge tourist attraction."

"Well, there's always the Detention Center," I joked, but Meg wasn't in a mood to appreciate my attempt at humor. Okay, then, I'd get serious. I fortified myself with a long drink of steaming coffee before posing the question that had kept me awake. "Meg—what do you think that guy was looking for?"

"I wish I knew. Did you think I was lying to Hanover?"

"Of course not. But you'd been knocked unconscious. You had trouble remembering what had just happened. Now that you've slept on it, doesn't anything come to mind? Something Kev or Pete may have mentioned even casually?"

"They were so busy I hardly saw them. And Pete . . . well, it sounds terrible to say now, but the truth is I was happier when I didn't see him."

"I know he wasn't one of your most favorite people. . . ." I began.

She didn't respond right away. When she did, the intensity and bitterness in her voice startled me. "He was my least favorite person. Whatever this is about, you can bet your bank account Pete Reilly was neck-deep in it!"

I was too shocked to point out that there was nothing in my account to bet. "You never said . . . when I asked you if there was trouble between Kev and Pete, if they'd argued, you said—"

"This isn't about Kev and Pete. It's about me and Pete."

"I never guessed you felt that way."

"Neither did Kev."

"Is it because of the fraud thing, or is there something else?"

"There were lots of things. I told you Pete never bothered to go up to Danbury to see Kev. And Kev wasn't gone two weeks before he was coming on to me."

I drew in my breath. "Didn't Kev—"

"I never told Kev. He had enough to cope with."

"But knowing all that, why'd you let Kev go into business with him again?"

"I couldn't stop it. He loved Pete. Their parents are dead. Pete was the little brother, his whole family. He couldn't see the kind of man he'd become."

"But he went to jail because of what Pete did."

"Oh, Carrie. If anyone should know about loving someone blindly . . ."

That stopped me. Because if they offered prizes for blind, I'd be up for the Academy Award.

"Sorry," Meg said, catching my expression. "That was a low blow."

"It's okay."

"It wasn't that Pete wasn't likable. He was a con man. Charm oozed out of his pores. You saw that."

I nodded.

"But he was . . . totally amoral. Nothing was ever right or wrong. Everything was shades of gray. I really don't believe he knew the difference."

We were quiet, eating our muffins without tasting them. Then Meg went on.

"I used to think he was evil. But he wasn't. He was just completely self-centered. If things went wrong it was always somebody else's fault. If Pete wanted something he took it. If other people got hurt in the process, well, that's just the way it had to be. He'd smile and come up with some platitude like 'you can't make an omelet without breaking eggs,' stuff like that. Like that was supposed to make it all right."

I downed more hot coffee, but I felt cold inside.

"Pete could look you straight in the eye and tell you something you knew was a lie," Meg continued. "If you faced him with it, he'd just twist the story around so you couldn't pin him down, even though you knew what he was doing. The terrible thing was he'd end up believing he'd gotten away with it. And most of the time, he did."

"Not this time."

"No. But Kev's paying too. Again."

So Pete wasn't the innocent victim. It put a whole new slant on things. What if Kev had found out about Pete? Could he have killed the brother he'd loved? I shook off the thought. Banion's scenario was more palatable. And more plausible considering what had happened last night. I still hadn't mentioned the mob connection to Meg, but she must be thinking Pete had been involved in something criminal. He certainly seemed the type to have gotten in bed with the mob. If Pete had stolen some of their money, Kev would never be safe until they were paid off. The use of the machete was obviously a fear tactic. A dagger or a bullet would've done as well.

"Meg . . ."

"What?"

"I wouldn't mention how you felt about Pete to the cops."

"I'm not stupid."

I changed the subject. "Was Pete ever married?"

"Oh, yeah. There're two ex-wives. Maxie put up with him for three years. They divorced after she caught him in bed with the other one, Kate, Something-or-other. A cokehead. They were married for only six months. Last I heard, Kate was in a sanitarium up in Maine."

Recalling Banion's mention of the drug-running deal, I asked, "Was he into drugs?"

"Marijuana. I don't think he did the heavier stuff, but I wouldn't swear to anything where Pete was concerned."

"No children."

"None we're aware of."

I cast a quick glance in Officer Fleming's direction. He still had one egg and several sausages to go.

"You've got to go over in your mind everything that happened this past week."

Before she bent her head, I saw the distress in her eyes. "I've tried. I can't seem to . . ."

I reached for her hand. "I know it's painful, but maybe you saw something, maybe Kev said something that didn't seem important at the time—"

And then she was angry, pulling her hand away. "Christ, Carrie, you're as bad as Hanover. Stop badgering me! Why won't you believe I can't remember? The whole week's a blur." She pressed her hands against her forehead as though by the action itself she could prod her sluggish brain. After a moment she looked at me and helplessly shook her head. "Maybe in time something'll come to me."

"Yeah, sure." Trouble was, people were getting killed. Time was a luxury we didn't have.

"Let's deal with today," Meg said. "We have to find a place to stay. I've been thinking of asking Jon to put us up."

So it was "Jon" now. I broke off a piece of muffin, smeared some jelly on it, and took a huge bite, more to give myself time to think than because I was still hungry. I chewed slowly, took another sip of coffee, and lowered my voice. "I really don't think that's a good idea. I'm not making any accusations, but Jonathan Olsen was the only one who knew we planned to be out last night—"

"Oh, come on, Carrie. I heard the killer's voice. It wasn't Jonathan's."

"He could've disguised it."

"And he could be the Phantom of the Opera underneath that Prince Charming mask, but I doubt it. Besides, Springer knows Jonathan knew where we were last night, and I'm sure he's talked to him. Jon must have an airtight alibi, because if the cops were suspicious, they'd be holding him."

"I'd still rather find someplace else to stay. Maybe Banion knows someone . . ."

"Carrie, he's a stranger. We can't impose on him."

Thinking about Sy Banion, I suddenly remembered his telling me he'd had people watching the B&B to protect Meg. Where the hell had they been last night? How safe would she be at the race on Sunday if the FBI couldn't manage a simple stakeout? They guy had some explaining to do. Telling Meg who Banion was on the tip of my tongue, but just then Officer Fleming's lanky figure loomed over us.

"Ready, ladies?"

"Gotta pay the check," I said, reaching into my bag.

"I'll get it," Meg said. And as Fleming walked away, she whispered, "You can stay with Banion if you want. I'll feel more comfortable at Jonathan's."

"Oh, nice," I hissed back. "That's real nice. I'll just take myself off and leave you alone with a possible suspect, who might feed you to his eel."

While she figured the tip, I surreptitiously pulled out Banion's card along with my lipstick and compact and stuck it in my pocket. I gave my reflection a quick glance, shuddered, and swiped at my lips. "No point in scaring the natives more than absolutely necessary," I muttered.

I caught up with Fleming just outside the restaurant. "Is there a hospital near here? I think Mrs. Reilly should have her head rebandaged."

"There's the Truman Medical Center."

Gingerly, Meg touched her head. "You know how ER's are. I'd just as soon not wait around. I'll be okay if we just stop someplace where I can make a call and pick up peroxide and gauze pads."

It had been in my mind to call Simon while Meg was occupied with the medics. "I don't know. Let me take a look."

She bent her head. There was a lump on her scalp the size of a paperweight, but the cut wasn't deep, so she was probably right. Fleming drove us to a large drugstore, and while Meg was making her purchases, he asked me what we'd decided.

"I think we may be staying with a friend," I said. But the more I thought about it, the more I was hoping Meg wouldn't be able to reach Jonathan. Banion might have access to safe houses. If he refused to let me tell Meg who he was, I'd tell her he had friends here in Key West who would lend us their place. I was about to run into the store to call, when Meg came out carrying a paper bag.

"Jon said he'd be happy to have us," she said as she climbed into the car. And to Fleming, "Would you take us to 622 Angela Street, please?"

I sighed and caved in. I'd go along with staying at Jonathan's, but only to avoid ending up as Springer and Hanover's overnight guests and only until I could get in touch with Banion. I stared out the window at the ocean and thought about Hanover's T-shirt with the predatory shark pursuing those terrified bluefish, who in reality wouldn't have had a chance in hell. And I thought about Snowy, the eel, and how much I didn't want to sleep in the same house with him. Don't get me wrong, I like eel.

It's just that I prefer it on rice, smoked and wrapped in seaweed, with me doing the eating.

JONATHAN WAS WAITING FOR us as we pulled up in front of his terra-cotta shuttered house. This morning he was wearing jeans and a yellow T-shirt that displayed every rippling muscle. I admit it bothered me to think a mob hit man might reside in that magnificent package. One lock of white-blond hair fell across his forehead, and his eyes shone with warmth. The warmth turned to concern as he took in Meg's bandaged head.

"You didn't tell me you'd been hurt."

If he'd done the deed, he was certainly the Laurence Olivier of perps.

"It's nothing. Carrie's going to change the bandage, and after I get some rest, I'll be fine."

"It's nice of you to let us stay here, Jonathan," I said formally. "It won't be for long. I have a friend who may know of something—"

"You can stay as long as you like. I've got plenty of room. I'm just glad you caught me before I took off for the day." He grabbed our suitcase, took Meg's arm, and led her inside. I thanked Officer Fleming and followed them. Jonathan's eyes stayed on Meg as he talked to me. "Your foot seems much better, Carrie. You're not limping."

The guy must have eyes on the back of his head. "To tell the truth, I forgot about it with everything that's happened."

He didn't ask for explanations. I assumed Meg had filled him in on the phone.

"You might want to shower and change," he said solicitously. "There're towels in the bathroom."

Sea World assaulted my eyes as we crossed through the living room to get to the bedroom area. In my exhausted state, just looking at all that underwater life was enough to give me vertigo. Snowy slithered out from his cave as I passed and—I swear to God—stuck out his tongue.

The room where Jonathan deposited our suitcase was small and inviting. There were twin beds covered with blue-and-white-checked comforters, an antique maple chest with brass fittings, on which he'd placed a vase filled with dried cornflowers, and a maple rocking chair in the corner. I was relieved to see that pastel florals, not seascapes, decorated the walls.

I eyed the beds longingly.

"The bathroom's right next door. You want to rest, or do you have to go somewhere?"

"I'd like to clean up," I said. "Then, as soon as I change Meg's bandage, I'm going to crash."

"I'm an EMT. I'll do the bandage," he said, and was unrolling the gauze before I could protest. "Want to talk about it?" he asked Meg.

"Please, no. I've gone over it so many times with the police, I'd just like to try and forget for now."

He didn't push her. I hovered over him, saw that his touch was gentle and that he worked quickly and efficiently. He was finished in half the time it would have taken me.

"Nice job," I said grudgingly.

"All in a day's work," he shrugged, bestowing on me one of those irresistible smiles.

I caught myself relenting, smiling back.

Get a grip, girl, I told myself, and reached for the suitcase.

"Thank you," Meg said to him. "Now, don't worry about us. You go do whatever you have to. We'll probably just try and catch up on sleep most of the day."

He dropped a key on the dresser. "I'll bring something back for dinner, then. Help yourselves to whatever you find in the fridge."

"Would you mind if I make a couple of calls?" I asked. "We're supposed to touch base with the police, and I have a credit card for long distance."

"Feel free. By the way . . ." He paused in the doorway. "I had a rather uncomfortable visit from the law myself earlier this morning."

Meg started to apologize for having mentioned his name to Hanover. I got very busy unpacking the few things I'd tossed into the suitcase.

"Good thing I spent last evening with friends who were able to vouch for my whereabouts," Jonathan said. "Otherwise I guess I'd've been in deep shit." A wave and he was gone.

A minute later we heard the door close behind him.

"Satisfied?" Meg said.

"I suppose." I looked around. "Isn't it nice we have the place to ourselves, though."

She regarded me suspiciously. "Why?"

Too late, I attempted to extract my foot. "Just that we won't have to go over everything till we've had a chance to get some rest."

Meg knew me better. "No snooping. I mean it, Carrie. Jon was kind enough to take us in. The least we can do is show him a little trust."

But I have a problem with trust.

AFTER I SHOWERED AND changed, I crawled under the blue-and-white-checked comforter, and within minutes I was gone. When I opened my eyes hours later, Meg was still asleep. Groggily, I glanced at my watch. Ten past one. I sat up, wondering for a split second where I was, if it was A.M. or P.M. Then the events of the past night struck me like a blow on the chest and I fell back against the pillow, longing to sink into oblivion for just a while longer. No luck. Ugly images crowded my mind. Up and around was preferable to dealing with ghosts. Taking care not to make noise, I slid into my sneakers and tiptoed out into the hall.

I decided to make my phone calls from the kitchen so I wouldn't disturb Meg. Besides, my stomach was rumbling. Jonathan had said to help ourselves to anything in the fridge. Knowing bachelors, I guessed I'd probably have a choice of stale bread and peanut butter, or last week's leftover pizza.

I had to cross through the living room to get to the kitchen. Involuntarily, my gaze was drawn to Snowy's cage. He gave me the evil eye and lashed his tail as I sidled past. That eel didn't like me. I started wondering what, besides rebellious slaves, comprised the creature's diet. Did Jonathan feed it live mice or fuzzy little ducklings? My skin crawled.

Watched by a thousand fishy eyes, I moved away from the cage, opened the door to the kitchen, and stopped short. I was gazing upon a *House Beautiful* white-on-white homemaker heaven, with sparkling copper pots and utensils hung over the center island, Sabatier knives in a rack next to the cooktop, and spices I never even heard of lined up—alphabetically yet—on a shelf above the stainless-steel sink. Not exactly what I would have envisioned for the Marlboro Man who'd picked me up at the airport. I would've guessed his tastes ran more toward cracked mugs and hot plates. Was it possible he was that happy combination: the strong but sensitive type, every woman's dream man?

I hopped on one of the high stools by the island, dug in my pocket for Simon's card, and dialed. I expected to get the front desk at Pier House, but instead heard a recorded male voice. "Please leave your name and number and your call will be returned."

"Mr. Banion . . . Simon," I whispered into the mouthpiece. "This is Carrie Carlin. Maybe you've heard by now, there's been another . . . incident. I can't have you calling me where I am, but I must talk to you. It's urgent. I'll try to reach you later today." I hung up quickly, cocked an ear toward the bedroom area. All quiet. Helping myself to some plump red grapes and a banana from a fruit bowl sitting in the center of the island, I punched in my credit-card number and dialed Ruth-Ann's apartment. She answered on the first ring.

I kept my tone light. I planned to keep everything on a "need to know" basis. "Hi, Ruth-Ann. Glad I caught you home. How're the cats?"

"Fine. I hope you don't mind, I brought them to my apartment."

"I appreciate it. It's better for them to be with you, even if it means staying inside for a few days. Everything else okay?"

There was what is known as a pregnant pause on the other end of the line.

"Ruth-Ann? Is everything okay?"

"Didn't Lieutenant Brodsky call you?"

"No. I was going to call him after—" She was answering my question with a question. "Why are you asking me that?"

"I've been trying to get you. Something happened—"

"Oh, God, something's happened to Allie or Matt!" The banana slipped through my fingers and fell, *splat,* onto the white tile floor. "Who broke something? Where are they? What hospital—"

"No, no, they're okay."

"Is it my father?"

"Everybody's fine. It's . . . *Meg's Place* was broken into last night." She whispered her reply, as though saying it out loud would make it more real.

I was so relieved that my family was intact, I had to stop myself from saying, "Is *that* all!"

"I tried to call you at that bed and breakfast, but some man answered and said you weren't staying there anymore."

"No, we're at a friends. How bad was it? What was stolen?"

"You know Franny from Golden Oldies?"

"Yes," I said impatiently, "she's running the café while Meg's down here."

"Well, Franny said she wasn't sure, but it didn't look like much of anything was missing. Meg's photographs are okay, and they didn't even bother with the artwork or the consignment antiques."

"Just the money from the register?"

"That's what's so weird. Franny said it's all there."

Meg's apartment at the B&B flashed in front of me, and suddenly I knew this wasn't your average run-of-the-mill break-in. These guys weren't looking for small change. They were after the pot of gold.

"They made a terrible mess," Ruth-Ann went on. "Franny called me when she couldn't reach Meg 'cause she thought I'd know where you were. The police are there, and they want her to close the café till Meg gets back."

I tore a piece of paper towel from a wooden roller, snagged the now-squashed banana, and rear-ended the door shut. "Have you been over there?"

"Not yet. I don't want to go while the police are around, but I promised Franny I'd help her clean up after they leave." Ruth-Ann avoids anyone wearing a uniform. The fear was bred into her bones by her Holocaust-survivor parents. She tolerates Ted, but that's because he doesn't wear a uniform and, as a result of past events, she's come to think of him as a sort of knight in plain clothes.

"I'm going to try to reach Lieutenant Brodsky. I'll call you later." I hung up before she had a chance to say anything else. I'd hardly replaced the receiver when the phone rang.

I answered it with some trepidation. "Hello?"

"Carrie? You all right?"

Ted's voice. Daybreak after a dark night, as I momentarily fell prey to the archaic reaction: This man will make everything all right. I tried to sound matter-of-fact. "I was about to call you," I said. "I just got off the phone with Ruth-Ann. She told me—"

"I've been trying you at the B&B," he interrupted. "Springer filled me in on what happened last night and gave me your number. Where are you?"

"At Jonathan's."

"Olsen? The guy who found Peter?"

"We had no place else to go."

"What's wrong with a hotel?"

"Everything's booked because of the races. Did Springer tell you that I . . . um . . ." I hesitated.

"That you what?"

"That I was the one who found the . . . body?"

I heard the beginnings of an expletive turned into a cough. "He neglected to mention that. Seems to be your karma, doesn't it?"

"Don't make jokes. It's not funny."

"No shit."

Pregnant pauses seemed to be the order of the day.

"Tell me what happened at Meg's Place," I said finally.

"There was a break-in."

"I know that much. I think it may all be related."

"Explain."

"Well, Ruth-Ann said Franny didn't think anything valuable was taken."

"It's out of my jurisdiction, but I'll find out."

"It . . . sounds like they were searching for something."

"Any idea what?"

"Maybe money. Not cash-register stuff. Big money. They were looking for something here too. The landlady just got in the way."

This pause was fraught with all sorts of danger signals.

"Has it crossed your mind that you also might be in the way? That that could've been you last night?"

Springer's words. I didn't want to be reminded.

"Come home, Carrie. Bring Meg with you. You're in over your heads."

I lowered my voice. "Meg won't leave till she knows what's happened to Kev. Springer won't let her anyway."

"Then come alone, damn it."

"I can't."

"What about the kids? Aren't they due back soon?"

"Not till Monday. I have a return flight out of here Monday morning. Come hell or high water, I'll be on it."

"You may be in for both."

"What?"

"Hell *and* high water."

I heard him saying something to someone in the background, followed by a familiar bark.

"Is that Horty? You've got him there at the precinct?"

The growl that came through the phone wasn't coming from a canine throat. "Goddamm it, Carrie, you are a pain in my ass. I'm flying down."

My heart gave a flutter. Annoyed with myself, I snapped at him. "There's really no need—"

"I think there is."

"What about the Smithline thing?" I asked, recalling the case he'd been working on.

"Wrapped up."

"But you have Horty—"

"If Ruth-Ann can't take him, the guys here will look after him. He's been practically living here anyhow."

I gave it one last shot. "I don't see what you can do—"

"Oh, shut up. The mountain's coming to Muhammad. Revel in it. See you." And he hung up.

Revel in it? "Arrogant bastard," I muttered as I replaced the receiver, trying my best not to be pleased that he cared enough to take time off to help me out. Actually, I was pleased on more than one count. It would be great having his enigma-solving brain around to pick. To say nothing of his body. I began fantasizing about a night of coitus *un*interruptus, then, ashamed to be thinking such thoughts at this particular time, brought my attention back to the matter at hand. Ted would have access to information that would be off-limits to Meg and me. But his being here complicated things too. I couldn't hold out on him face to face. Whether Banion liked it or not, I'd have to tell Ted that I'd been to Christopher House and about the FBI's involvement. There was no denying he'd be on my case to back off and leave things to the professionals. And where would he stay? Jon had only one extra bedroom. Plus, we couldn't impose a perfect stranger on him, especially not one who, by profession, was an even bigger snoop than I am.

Thinking about snooping reminded me of my dishonorable intentions. I dropped the banana in the garbage pail that I found stowed away under the sink, sneaked back through the living room—avoiding glancing at Snowy's cage—and crept to our bedroom door. I opened it and peeked in. Meg was still asleep. I backed out, closed the door, and went down the hall to Jonathan's room.

The door was closed, but it opened easily when I turned the handle. A point in his favor. With strangers in the house, a person who had something to hide would probably have locked his door. I paused on the threshold, my eyes taking in the small room. Color scheme: monochromatic beige. An extralong queen-size bed, made up with an off-white chenille spread. A teakwood dresser, on which were a comb and brush and a couple of disk cases, but no pictures. A computer on a computer desk with a book opened next to it, and a bookshelf on which, neatly arranged, were a dozen or so books framed by a pair of bronze dolphin bookends. An aquarium stood on a long table beneath the window. Other than sea plants, it seemed to contain no life.

I picked up the book that was open next to the

computer. It was a textbook having to do with mollusks and reptiles. No surprise there. I glanced at the titles of the books on the shelf. Except for a couple of computer manuals and a dictionary, all were work-related. I opened the closet. Pants and a few jackets, one blue suit covered in plastic—obviously rarely worn—several shirts, a couple of pairs of sneakers, boots, diving gear, snorkeling equipment. Nothing different from what I would have expected. I pulled open his dresser drawers and rummaged around, being careful not to disturb the order. Calvin Klein briefs, athletic socks, T-shirts, and shorts neatly folded. No pajamas. This man either slept in his briefs or—not. I gave the image thirty seconds, then let it go.

Just the desk drawers left. As I was about to pull one open, I had the sensation that there was movement in the aquarium, but a closer examination revealed only ferns, some coral, and rocks. I surmised the movement came from bubbles from the water hose, which I assumed Jonathan kept going for the vegetation. I wondered why he didn't put a few fish in the tank, for color if nothing else.

On my way back to the desk, I passed the bathroom, opened the door, and was surprised to see a darkroom. I noticed a stack of photographs on a ledge beside the double sink and began flipping through them. Stunningly beautiful shots of underwater marine life—a world of mystery and incredible color. Was there anything this guy couldn't do? No wonder he was attracted to Meg. They were both "golden" children.

I was fascinated, mesmerized, only partway through the stack, when like the bubbles exploding up from the depths of the aquarium, it came to me—what the killer might have been searching for! *Meg's* photographs, the ones she'd been taking the day of the murder. If I was right the possibility existed that, without knowing it, Meg had the killer on film. Or at least the killer believed she did. Where were those photographs? Probably not even developed. Where was the film, then? Had Meg sent it to Franny at the café, planning to develop it when she got home? Was that why the café had been searched? Or was it still at the B&B? Probably not. If the killer had found what he was looking for in Meg's rooms, the café wouldn't have been ransacked. So it followed that Meg must still have the film.

I flew out of the darkroom, remembering to close Jonathan's door behind me, and dashed down the hallway through the living room to our bedroom.

"Meg, wake up!" I shook her and she came awake instantly.

"What happened? Is it Kev? Have they found Kev?"

"No. No, I'm sorry." Seeing her terror, I was filled with remorse. "I didn't mean to scare you, but Meg, I think I know what the killer was looking for."

"What are you talking about?"

"The film, the film. The photos you took the day of the accident. You must've caught him on film. If I'm right he killed to get it and he'll do it again. Where is it? What did you do with the film?"

She stared at me blankly.

I sat by her on the bed, took both her cold hands in mine, and in my excitement practically crushed them. "What did you do with the film you took that day?"

"I . . . I don't know."

My voice came out in a screech. "You don't know?"

"I don't remember. I'm sure I must've taken it out of the camera. I may have put it in the carrying case, or maybe I put it in my handbag . . ."

"They looked in your bag. They dumped it out on the floor. They dumped the case too. What were you wearing?"

"What was I wearing?" She withdrew her hands, got off the bed, and fumbled around in her bag for a cigarette.

I chewed my knuckles in an effort to keep my mouth shut as she lit it and began pacing around the small room. I knew Meg felt she thought more clearly with a cigarette in her hand. She took a drag, blew the smoke out through her nose, and as I watched it curl in a lazy stream toward the ceiling, my father's words when I was fourteen and experimenting came back to me. *"Women who smoke look like dragons."* Not men, women. If I said such an antifeminist thing to my daughter today, she'd do a pack a day just to spite me.

"Hope this isn't a smoke-free zone," Meg murmured, flashing me a rueful half-smile.

"Think, Meg. Maybe you stuck it in a pocket? If you did—"

"My khaki shorts and the green tee with *The Megan* on it."

"Do you remember if you put it in the pocket?"

"I don't know. It's a blank. That whole couple of days. From the minute the police called, it's like someone took an eraser and wiped those days off my memory."

"Could you have mailed the film home?"

"No, I don't think so. When would I have done that? *Why* would I do that? Oh, God, what's wrong with me? Why can't I remember?"

I tried to mask my frustration. "Never mind. It's a perfectly normal reaction. Nature's way of helping you cope. It'll come back."

"But I need to remember now."

"Don't worry. We'll think of something."

She sat on the edge of the bed and I started pacing. I knew that as long as the killer or killers thought we could identify them, we'd never be safe. Not here in Key West or back home in Norwood or Piermont. My eyes lit on Meg's camera sitting next to my laptop in the corner of the room, and as I went to pick it up, my synapses started connecting. Normal reaction, abnormal reaction, *ab*reaction! I remembered when Ruth-Ann was doing alpha-theta training for her eating addiction and suddenly the repressed memory of the rape became as vivid as though it were happening in the present. Could I help Meg to bring up a repressed memory? She was imaginative, an excellent visualizer. What could we lose by trying? I'd hook her up, bring her into an alpha state, watch for the theta crossover, and see if anything surfaced. Clutching the laptop, I whirled around. "Would you be willing to try a little experiment?"

"Anything."

My hands were shaking as I placed the computer on the night table and started uncoiling the wires. "Maybe, just maybe, the gods'll smile on us and this will work."

"What? What're you talking about?"

"Lie down on the bed and try to relax. We're going to do a little alpha-theta training."

'M NOT A HYPNOTHERAPIST. Alpha-theta training isn't hypnosis. It's a form of self-regulation where the subject puts himself into a deeply relaxed meditative state, turning the thoughts inward. Monks work for years to attain high levels of the alpha brain wave. Athletes and astronauts practice alpha-theta training to enhance peak performance. For most people it takes many sessions to achieve a theta crossover, the state in which the levels of the theta brain wave are greater than the alpha. In this state a person becomes suggestible; it's when I teach my patients "self talk" to overcome negative thinking. Sometimes, as in Ruth-Ann's case, a client achieves self-healing through a re-living of a past traumatic experience. But it's touchy, digging into a person's subconscious. I'm not a psychiatrist, and I wasn't entirely confident about playing Dr. Freud with my friend's head.

I was hoping to bring Meg into a state of what we call passive sensory awareness, thus allowing her to focus inwardly. I wasn't certain whether or not, for our purposes, anything useful might come of it, but our killer was getting antsy. Antsy killers make me antsy. I don't like to be within firing—or, in this case—machete range. At best, with coaching from me, Meg might be able to fill in the blanks of that terrible day. At worst we'd be exactly where we were now.

It helped that over the past year Meg had had several sessions of alpha-theta training, but her focus then had been on peak performance to heighten creativity. What I was about to ask her to do now was something neither of us had ever tried before.

I found a boom box on a bookshelf in the living room, lugged it into the bedroom, and plugged in a tape. I'm in the habit of keeping tapes in my laptop carrying case, which was fortunate, because Jonathan didn't strike me as the type to have anything resembling "Healing Waterfall" or Pachelbel's Canon in his CD collection. Of course, I could be wrong. I was discovering that he was a man of wide-ranging tastes.

Meg was leaning back against the pillows with her

eyes already closed. Since the accident I had assiduously avoided water imagery with her, but today I was going for broke. I attached the electrodes to her earlobes and to the crown of her head and flipped in a diskette. I determined her optimal alpha-theta protocol, turned up the music, and after guiding her through a brief muscle-relaxation exercise, sent her off on a sensory voyage to . . . I knew not where.

"Meg," I began in my singsong monotone, "every sensation, every experience you've ever had is forever recorded in your brain. You have the ability to relive those sensations and experiences as vividly as when they originally occurred. You're going to reconstruct now a scene in your mind's eye of the day you last saw Kev and Pete." I paused, crossed my fingers, and plunged on. "You're on the beach. You're wearing your khaki shorts and the green shirt with the picture of Kev's boat on it. You're carrying your camera equipment. Feel the wind on your face. Hear the screeching of the gulls and the pelicans overhead. It's a misty, overcast day. The spray from the ocean is like tiny needles on your face and arms as the wind whips up the water. Look up at the sky now. It's gray. You can't see the sun because it's hiding behind a thundercloud. Look out to sea. The water is a dark midnight blue dotted with whitecaps. Listen to the beating of the waves, the crashing back and forth, back and forth of the water against the shore. With each wave that laps against the shore, you become more and more relaxed, go deeper and deeper into memory." I fixed my eyes on the computer readout and was silent, allowing the music and the auditory feedback from the software to take over.

In less than fifteen minutes I saw the theta crossover.

"Where are you, Meg?" I began very softly.

"Down at the pier," she whispered, "at Fury Dock."

Fury Dock. Appropriately named, this place of watery death.

"Tell me what you see."

"I'm watching *The Megan.*"

"What's happening?"

"I can barely make it out. I can't see Kev and Pete at all. It's so hazy, and the wind is whipping up the spray—fogging my lens. I'm cleaning it off, using my zoom." When she spoke again her voice was breathy, high-pitched with excitement. "They're magnificent. It's like they're flying, hydroplaning the surface."

"Are they alone or are they racing someone?"

"Alone." Her voice dropped to a whisper. "Like a ghostly silver streak shrouded in mist."

I felt chilled by the words, but pushed on. "Can you see any other boats?"

"A couple of fishing boats coming in and . . . a schooner being whipped around by the wind, trying to haul in the sails."

"Anyone on the beach?"

A long pause.

"I can see a young couple wearing white bikinis down near the water, but they're getting up and leaving. They're trying to fold up their towels, but the wind is too strong."

"Anything else?"

"A man wearing a straw hat's trying to close his beach umbrella and hang on to his hat at the same time."

"Where're Kev and Pete now? Can you still see them?"

"They're swinging around. Heading in."

This was new. Had Kevin and Pete docked the boat before Meg left and then decided to go back out?

"Do you see Jonathan's boat?"

"There's a dinghy a little ways off. Rocking on the waves."

"Anyone in it?"

"No."

"What are you doing?"

"Still shooting."

"Where's *The Megan?*"

"They've pulled into a slip. I don't know why they've come in. There doesn't seem to be anything wrong with the boat."

The music stopped suddenly as the tape ran out, and fearful the mood would be broken, I hit the rewind, waited, then pressed PLAY again. I kept my voice soft and flat, certain we were finally getting to something important.

"What are the guys doing now?"

"Pete's jumped onto the dock. I think he's talking to the man with the hat. Kev's in the cockpit." Her voice quivered. "He sees me. I've caught him waving to me."

I waited a few seconds. "Are you going down to the dock?"

"The wind's knocked the tripod over. I'm packing up, signaling to Kev and Pete that I'm leaving."

"Have you shot the whole roll of film?"

"Yes."

"Have you taken it out of the camera?"

"Yes."

"Where are you putting it?"

An eternity later. "I'm wedging it in the tripod."

Excitement prickled my skin, but on its heels came dismay. Meg had left the beach before Kev and Pete took the boat back out. She would have nothing on film of the events that had immediately preceded the accident. Why then would the killers have been so eager to get their hands on it? Maybe my deduction had been wrong.

Meg fell silent, and as I allowed the tape to play out, I gradually brought her back to a more externally focused state.

On the count of ten she opened her eyes. "It's in the tripod," she said breathlessly.

"I know."

She sat up. "That's back at the B&B. Let's—"

"It isn't going to help us."

"What do you mean?"

"You left the dock before the guys went back out."

"But if you're right the killer wants it enough to kill for it," Meg said. "There must be something on it, something I shot that I'm not remembering."

"Unless I was wrong about the film being what they're after."

The loud jangle of the phone made us both jump. Automatically, I reached for it.

"Hello?"

"Carrie?"

"Simon!" I saw Meg's brow furrow at the mention of Banion's name. My own relief at hearing his voice was tinged with bewilderment. I hadn't left this phone number on the tape. How had he known where to find me?

"One of my men followed the patrol car this morning," he said as though I'd asked.

"Then you must've heard what happened last night—"

"Don't worry, we're on top of it. Can you talk?"

Don't worry? A woman was killed! Meg was attacked! Where the hell was his man when that was going on? But Meg was sitting two feet away. I choked back my anger, managed to keep my voice level. "No, I can't. And I think it's time you and Meg talked."

Meg shot me an irritated look that said louder than words what she thought of that suggestion.

"I'll get to that." Banion's voice was strained, his tone sharper than it had been the previous evening. I guess if I were FBI and someone had gotten whacked on my watch, I'd be a tad tense too.

"Things are moving faster than we expected. Whether or not she's aware of it, Meg Reilly has something the mob wants. She was taking pictures the day of the accident. Could there be something on them?"

So maybe I was right! "I don't know."

"It's essential you find out."

"I'm . . . not sure that's possible."

"Make it possible, before something worse happens."

Worse than two murders? Then with a jolt I realized what he meant.

"What does he want, for heaven's sake?" Meg hissed impatiently.

I covered the mouthpiece and lied. I was getting better at it. "He's offering to put us up." I'd begun walking around in nervous little circles and forced myself to sit on the bed. "Thanks for the offer," I said into the phone, "but we've decided to bunk with a friend of Meg's. We're wiped out. We need time to—"

"We're running out of time. I don't know how much longer we can protect you."

I have a friendly old hound dog that could protect us better than you have, I thought.

"I'll . . . uh . . . discuss it with Meg. I'll get back to you."

"I'll come by tomorrow and explain everything to

Mrs. Reilly." He hung up before I could reply. I looked at Meg and forced a smile.

"He wants to help."

"Why? Why is a complete stranger interested in getting involved in this at all?"

"Maybe he's just a concerned citizen," I hedged feebly, cursing Simon under my breath.

"Oh, give me a break. He's a nut, a voyeur, like those people who can't stay away from fires." She got up and started rummaging around in the suitcase, found a clean shirt and a pair of shorts. "How'd he know we were here anyway?"

"I think the cops are giving out this phone number, but not the address." I was congratulating myself on that equivocation till Meg asked with her usual logic, "Why would they, when it could put us in danger?"

"Well, they certainly gave it to Ted." I took advantage of the opportunity to change the subject. "Did I tell you he called? He's flying down as soon as he can get a flight."

"He really cares about you, Carrie. That's rare. Don't mess things up."

"I know, but—"

"No buts. Don't make him pay for Rich."

One of the things that makes Meg so special is her grace under fire. She was concerned about me and my problems when her own life was in a shambles.

Speaking of Ted reminded me about the café. "Oh, God, there's something I forgot to tell you."

The expression on my face stilled her hands.

I hastened to reassure her. "There was a break-in at the café, but your insurance should cover the damage. No one was hurt and nothing was taken that Franny can figure. Not even cash."

"Nothing was taken? Hell, Carrie, can't you see it's connected? They were looking for the money or the film or whatever the hell it is they want." She drew in her breath. "That's why Ted's coming down, isn't it? He's worried about you."

"And about you."

"Maybe it *is* the film," she said after a minute.

"Maybe when they couldn't find it at Mrs. Larrabee's, they thought you'd sent it home," I said.

She nodded and was quiet, mulling over possibilities. Then she grabbed the clean clothes and headed for the bathroom, calling back over her shoulder, "I'm going to shower and change. Then we'll go get it."

Fifteen minutes later she was ready. We didn't think it through, didn't deal with the how-to's or our emotions at all, just picked up our tote bags, walked past the aquarium—studiously ignoring Snowy—and left the house.

We decided to walk. My ankle was much improved, and hot as it was, there was a breeze. I was glad to get out in the air. We kept a steady pace, talking little, jumpy as a couple of cats on a rubber raft, each reluctant to voice her fears to the other. Meg kept glancing over her shoulder. My eyes practically strip-searched everyone we saw. Most had on clothes so skimpy it would've been a miracle if they were concealing a weapon. Heading in our direction was a woman wearing very short shorts and no bra under a pink sleeveless knit shirt; she was walking a black poodle with matching pink bows on either ear. Behind her strolled a very blond young black woman in tight jeans and a cutoff shirt, her midriff bare. If they were toting guns, they'd've had to be the size of toothpicks. Across the street I saw a unisex group of tennis players, all in various forms of designer tennis whites, and two really great-looking guys in bikini bathing trunks and T-shirts, holding hands. No one stopped suddenly and stared into a shop window as I bent over to retie my tied shoelace. Nobody darted down a side street when Meg paused at the gate of the city cemetery.

"I haven't even thought about where Pete should be buried."

"It's not your decision. It's Kev's."

I was telling her I believed Kevin was alive, and she smiled gratefully.

I began to formulate plans to get us back into the apartment. On my wavelength, Meg said, "Have you thought about what we're going to say if the police are still there?"

"How about the truth?"

"You're kidding."

"Okay, a half-truth. We'll say you need your tripod. You're planning to do some work."

"Oh, sure. They'll buy that about as fast as they'll believe I've taken up boat racing."

"Why don't we just tell them we think something may be on the film?"

"No!"

Taken aback by her vehemence, I glanced at her sharply, but her eyes were resolutely fixed on the lady with the poodle who had stopped with her charge next to a fire hydrant.

"The police would confiscate it before I got a chance to develop it," she murmured. "I want to see it first."

Could Meg be harboring a suspicion that Kev actually was involved? I thought about Rich's words to me when he left. *Things happen. People change.* Suddenly I realized the truth of that, a concept I'd been fighting ever since he'd said it. People do change. Some for the better, some for the worse. Maybe prison had changed Kev. Hanover had said a member of a crime family was in Danbury at the same time Kev was there. Maybe Banion's informant had been off the mark and the mob connection had been Kev's, not Pete's.

Olivia Street was quiet as we rounded the corner and approached the white gable-roofed house. Maybe it was the sight of the yellow crime-scene tape wound around the porch railing, but all at once I was dragging my feet at the thought of seeing the rooms where Millie Larrabee had been so brutally murdered. I didn't want to go back into that apartment. I didn't want to see the chalk outline of her body the police had probably drawn on the floor, didn't want to see the pool of dried blood, the ransacked rooms, smell the stench of death.

Meg stopped beside me. "I can't go in there," she said. "I don't know how I thought I could. I don't know how we even slept there last night."

Meg had been the strong one when I needed her. I had to come through for her now. "Maybe the police've cleaned it up," I said, knowing that wasn't how things worked. I gritted my teeth to stop their chattering. "We have to get the film. You wait here. I'll go in."

How I was going to manage that, I hadn't figured out. We drew closer to the house and stared at the tape, a yellow plastic barrier as forbidding as if it were made of steel.

"Returning to the scene of the crime, ladies?" a familiar voice boomed from across the street.

I started and turned to see Detective Hanover lounging against the door of an unmarked car. He was wearing a brown cotton jacket over a lime green shirt decorated with a palm tree—not exactly haute couture, but a vast improvement over the shark with the humongous teeth. From where I stood, his expression didn't look any friendlier than it had last night.

Before I could open my fat mouth and tick him off, Meg had swung into action. She crossed the street and bestowed on him a wan but beatific smile. Reluctantly, I followed.

"I'm glad you're here, Detective," Meg was saying. "I've left a few things I need in my rooms. Could we go in?"

"Not possible," was the gruff reply. "Place's been cordoned off."

"You can come up with us," she said, "look over whatever we take."

"Sorry, no can do."

I was shocked to see tears spill over onto those pale cheeks, till I reminded myself of Meg's remarkable ability to cry on cue. *Hot damn,* I thought to myself, *the old Meg's back.*

"I only wanted one or two things—personal items, a few pictures of my husband—" Her voice caught, and suddenly I realized the tears flowing unheeded down her cheeks weren't an act.

The man was a robot. The stone face behind those horn-rimmed glasses registered no emotion. I picked up the ball, trying to keep my tone pleasant. "I can't imagine we could do any damage to the crime scene if we took some clothes and a few pictures."

"Doesn't matter what you imagine. Everything's evidence."

"Including our underwear?"

The second the words were out of my mouth I regretted them. I saw the smirk, suppressed the urge I'd had ever since I met this guy to push his face in. What was his problem? Was it just us, or was he obnoxious to everyone?

"Not up to me, anyway."

"Who is it up to?"

"You could start with the lieutenant."

"Okay. Could you call him?"

" 'Fraid not."

Chill, Carrie, I warned myself. *Do not lose your cool.* "Why is that?"

"He's already on his way here."

Why couldn't you say that in the first place, you creep? I thought. "Okay, we'll wait."

I took Meg by the arm and we crossed back to the other side, plopping ourselves down on the curb.

"Warms the cockles of your heart, doesn't he?" I commented, struggling to pull my shorts down in an attempt to avoid scorching my thighs. "Pity his wife if he's married. Imagine having to crawl into bed with that."

Meg grinned. "Oh, I don't know. Maybe underneath that crusty exterior lies the phallus of Lucky Pierre."

We dissolved into laughter. It was either that or scream as we sat there broiling in the blazing sun, perfect targets for whoever might feel like tossing a bullet or a machete our way. Hanover watched us from the air-conditioned comfort of his car, certain we'd taken leave of our senses. Calming down, I was suddenly fed up. Fed up with Hanover's surly attitude, fed up with Jonathan Olsen, fed up with Sy Banion's obsession with secrecy, fed up with everyone involved in this sordid mess working at cross-purposes. I'd keep Banion's secret for one more day as I'd promised, I decided, but by the time Ted got here, that particular jig was going to be up. Jonathan, on the other hand, wasn't getting another minute.

"Meg," I began, "did Kev or Pete ever mention a hotel called Christopher House to you?"

"I don't think so. Why?"

"Jonathan didn't want me to tell you, but I think you should know. The woman who called when he took the message said something about it being all set for New Year's Eve at Christopher House."

Meg looked startled. "What?"

"I checked last night to see if there were New Year's Eve reservations for a Reilly, but there weren't. There was a reservation for a K. Peters, and at first I thought—"

"Peters? There was a reservation for K. Peters?"

"Yeah, but—"

"Pete did that sometimes," Meg said, her voice rising with excitement. "Used his first name."

"Oh. Well, maybe he'd made the reservation planning that you'd all go there for—"

"No, no, it was a message to me from Kev!"

I studied her in dismay. Meg was seeing everything that happened as a sign that Kevin was alive and trying to contact her. I tried to undo the damage. "I don't think you should take this as—"

"Yes. Don't you see? He's telling me to meet him there on New Year's Eve. That's why he used his initial with Pete's name. Oh, my God, I knew he was alive. I told you . . ."

"Why wouldn't he make the reservation in his own name?" *For that matter,* I thought, *if he's alive why not just show up?*

"He's in hiding. He can't use his own name. I can't understand why Jon didn't want me to know something so important, something that proves—"

"I think *Jon* had a different take on it."

"What do you mean?"

Just then Springer pulled up behind Hanover's car, which saved me from having to explain exactly what Jonathan had thought the message meant. Come to think of it, what he'd led me to believe he thought it meant. So that I wouldn't tell Meg. Which I hadn't, till now.

Springer spoke briefly to Hanover, then crossed over to us. His manner was solicitous, which was such a change from Hanover that I felt like hugging him.

"How're you doing, Mrs. Reilly?" he inquired, extending his hand to Meg.

The excitement that had shown on Meg's face a minute ago was well-masked. "As well as can be expected, I guess, Lieutenant," she murmured. "I don't suppose there've been any developments?"

"Sorry, no. The autopsy results will take some time, and I'm afraid there's been no sign of your husband."

Meg nodded and looked away. I waited, hoping she would tell Springer about the message and what she deduced from it, but she remained obstinately silent. There was a painful pause, which I finally ended. "Did Detective Hanover tell you why we're here?"

"He said you wanted a few things from the apartment. It's not usual to let people back into a crime area, but I'll take you up."

I turned to Meg. "You don't need to come. I can get what you need."

"No," she said. "I'll be quicker. I know where things are."

Springer ducked under the tape and we followed. I squelched the impulse to thumb my nose at Hanover.

I kept my eyes fixed resolutely on my sneakers as we walked past the pastel sitting room, up the stairs, and through the ghost-inhabited living room to the bedroom. If there was a chalk outline near the kitchen, I made sure I didn't see it. As we made our way through the living room, the crunching sound of the broken Christmas ornaments under our feet was enough reminder of last night's horror. I began breathing through my mouth like a dog panting, fearful of the odors that would assail me. I felt as though invisible crime-scene tape were wound around my chest, squeezing the breath from my body. It was a relief to stand in the bedroom doorway beside Springer as he watched Meg rummage through the jumble of clothes on the floor and through the drawers of the dresser. She worked quickly, making a small pile on the bed of some underthings and several photographs.

"Have you seen a picture of the race boat, Lieutenant?" I asked, desperate to get his attention off Meg.

He shook his head. "Not in one piece."

I took one of the photographs from Meg's pile. It was a clear picture of both Kev and Pete sitting on the side of their raceboat, grinning broadly into the camera. Springer took his eyes off Meg long enough to study it, and out of the corner of my eye, I saw her take a few steps to the right, run her hands quickly over the tripod, then drop to her knees and pick up a blouse off the floor.

Springer turned back to Meg. "May I have this? I'll return it later."

"Of course," she replied. "I'm finished here. I think I have everything we'll need for a few days."

I held my breath as he did a quick search through the small pile on the bed. It was a stroke of luck that he didn't ask to examine the blouse Meg had draped over her arm. "Okay, let's go."

I picked up the pile of clothes, took the blouse from Meg, stuffed everything in my tote bag, and a minute later we were outside, gratefully gulping in mouthfuls of fresh air. We thanked Springer, ignored Hanover, and headed to the corner, careful to walk slowly. I could sense Hanover's gaze on my back.

"You get it?" I whispered as we turned the corner and picked up our pace.

"In the blouse pocket."

"Good."

We didn't speak again till we were at the foot of the old cemetery and saw the black Ford. Two men were getting out as we approached. One was tall—well over six feet—sinewy-thin, and wore Dockers, a black T-shirt that showed off Evander Holyfield biceps, and a black baseball cap pulled down low, the peak shielding his face. The other was medium height, also wearing a black baseball cap, baggy jeans, and a jacket—odd attire for a day in which the temperature was hovering in the low eighties. His right hand was tucked inside his jacket. That, plus the fact that they quickened their pace when they saw us, brought me up short.

"Those men," Meg started to say. "I don't like—"

"In here!" I grabbed her, pushed her through the wrought-iron cemetery gate, and saw the men start to run.

Graveyards I have known normally don't provide much cover. Unless you're dead, of course, which I was trying my damnedest to keep us from being. This one was a hide-and-seeker's dream. Above-ground white concrete crypts were piled one on top of the other, and in among elaborately carved tombstones were a profusion of large mausoleums that resembled miniature houses, many adorned with fresh bouquets of bright flowers. Scattered among these were the flora and fauna of the tropics: leafy trees, poinciana, banyons, and red-leafed bushes that one would expect in a park rather than a cemetery. We darted in and out, tripping over stones and debris, glancing over our shoulders as we ran, ducking from time to time behind a tree or a three-tiered crypt to catch our breath.

We dashed down a path wedged between a high row of hedges and a large mausoleum with an arched roof crowned by a cross. To the side was a fenced-in area, over which was a Jewish star and a large sign reading, B'NAI ZION. No discrimination here. The arched, open doorway of the mausoleum beckoned us, but a group of about a half dozen tourists—all wearing yellow beanies—was gathered around chattering and laughing as though they were at Disneyland. A guide was standing in the doorway doing her thing. We dove into the hedge and squeezed next to the fence.

"In there," I hissed, "when they leave."

But the ladies weren't moving. They seemed fascinated by one of the markers on the tomb, taking endless pictures of one another standing in front of it.

"You see anything?" Meg whispered after several anxious minutes. "Did we lose them?"

I separated the bushes and peered out. Two black baseball caps were bobbing along the path running perpendicular to the B'nai Zion gate, stopping occasionally to conduct a more-thorough search of a particular structure. A couple of women, not part of the beanie group, glanced curiously at my face sticking out of the hedge. I dropped to my knees, pulling Meg down beside me, and began tracing an imaginary carved flower with my finger. "This'll make a wonderful rubbing," I said loudly enough for only them to hear. "Do you have the charcoal?"

From her prone position Meg began searching furiously in her tote bag. I looked up, saw the women coming toward us, and had a moment of panic thinking they were going to ask to see the nonexistent engraving. They were middle-aged, one tall and thin with short iron-gray hair, the other, small and hippy, wearing red flowered shorts.

Skinny smiled at me. "Excuse me . . ."

I tried to look busy and annoyed. "Yes?" I said shortly.

"I'm sorry to bother you, but would you mind taking our picture together?"

I cast a pleading glance in Meg's direction. She shrugged helplessly. "Uh . . ." I began. "I'm sorry, I'm really terrible with cameras."

"Oh, don't worry, this one's an idiot's delight," Skinny said. "You just push this button, and the camera does the rest."

Slowly, I got to my feet, my eyes desperately sweeping the area. As Meg looked on in silent agony, I took the camera in hands slippery with sweat and moved in a crouched-over stance—the camera in front of my face—away from the shelter of the hedge. The women followed and took up positions on either side of the archway. The yellow beanies moved off.

"Make sure you get the inscription," Flowered Shorts instructed.

I shot the fastest picture in history.

"Thanks," Skinny said. "Want me to take the two of you?"

I shook my head. "Doing rubbings," I gasped, and crawled on my hands and knees back to the hedge.

"Well, be sure you do Pearl's," she advised. "It's a hoot."

"Come on, Marge," Flowered Shorts called impatiently. "I want to see the naked, bound lady before we leave."

I didn't want to think about bound ladies, naked or otherwise.

"Look at the little lamb, Etta," I heard Marge exclaim. "It's a baby's grave. *Rebecca Elizabeth Johnson, 1891 to 1892. 'And the children of men take refuge in the shadow of Thy wings.'* "

"Amen," I muttered. As we dashed into the mausoleum, I heard running footsteps fading in the distance.

Our legs and shorts were filthy from kneeling on the gravel, and my heart threatened to burst out of my chest. The old "fight or flight" response I'm always teaching my patients to control.

Except in situations like this, I silently preached. *This is the time you need all the adrenaline you can pump. This is when flight is definitely the way to go.*

"They gone?" Meg's face was flushed, and we were both drenched through with sweat.

"I think so. I think they went through to the other side."

We peered out from the doorway, our eyes darting from tomb to tomb like a couple of hunted rabbits. "Come on," Meg whispered. "We'll double back and grab a cab."

It was a stroke of luck that we came on one parked by the curb almost as soon as we'd dashed out of the cemetery. The driver, a long-haired middle-aged hippie type, took in our frazzled, dirt-streaked appearance without comment.

The Ford was still parked where it had pulled up, its occupants nowhere to be seen.

"There's extra bucks in it if you get us to 622 Angela Street in three minutes," I gasped as we jumped in.

He looked at me as though I'd asked him to drive us to New York. "It's just around the corner. You can walk."

"My friend sprained her ankle," I snapped impatiently. "She's in pain."

He made it in two. I tossed him a ten spot. It was the best money I ever spent.

The brown Jeep was parked in front of the house, and Jonathan, his arms full of grocery bags, was letting himself in the front door as the cab rocketed around the corner and came to a screeching halt. When he saw us stumbling out of the backseat looking like a couple of refugees from a homeless shelter, he dropped the bags and was down the steps before the cab had shifted gears. I still had misgivings about this guy, but I swear to God, bounding down those steps, golden hair flying, muscles bulging, poised to slay any monsters—human or otherwise—that might be pursuing us, he looked like a combination of Whatshisname Van Damme and the Angel Gabriel. He asked no questions, just put a protective arm around each of us and shepherded us into the house.

"Sit." He pointed to the couch. "I'm going to fix you a drink that'll have you feeling no pain, and then you're going to tell me what happened."

"Don't mention the film," I whispered to Meg as we fell like two zombies onto the couch, sinking into its comforting, womblike warmth. I closed my eyes, but opened them when I felt the couch shaking. Meg was laughing so hard, tears were streaming down her cheeks.

"Relax," I said, patting her arm. "You're having a reaction, that's all."

"No, no," she giggled. "It's not that." She wiped her eyes, smudges of dirt streaking her cheeks. "Didn't you see it?"

"What?"

"The grave marker—why they all wanted their pictures taken by it."

"No, I was a little preoccupied," I said darkly.

"It said . . . it said . . ." Meg dissolved again.

"You're hysterical."

"No . . . no . . ." She got herself under control and wiped her eyes. "It said, *Pearl Roberts . . . 1929 to 1979.*"

"Oh, that's a real hoot," I commented. "I always laugh when I hear about people dying at fifty. At that rate, ten more years and I've had it."

"Let me finish," Meg said between giggles. "It said, *Pearl Roberts, 1929 to 1979. 'I told you I was sick.' *"

When Jonathan came back with our drinks, we were both doubled up, rolling around on the couch.

"Hey, hey," he said soothingly, as though he were talking to two inmates from the Bellevue psych ward. "It's okay, you're okay now. Here, drink." He held out a glass and I took it, gulped, and choked, brought out of my hysteria by the physical task of trying to breathe.

"What *is* that?" I wheezed when I could talk.

"Straight vodka. You needed it."

"Appreciate the thought, but next time warn me. I'm used to my booze diluted."

He grinned that grin. "Sorry, but I'll bet you're feeling better."

Meg was in better shape than I. She'd gotten herself under control and, forewarned by the deep honey color of the scotch Jonathan had handed her, was sipping it slowly. I left her to relate the saga of the cemetery while I made my way to the kitchen. I opened the fridge, found the bottle of tonic water he'd used to make my drink yesterday, and filled my glass to the top.

As I expected, spoons were neatly stacked next to

perfectly aligned forks and knives in a drawer next to the mirror-shiny stainless-steel sink. I stirred my drink, carefully washed the spoon, dried it, and returned it to its nest among its sister spoons. Either this guy never ate at home, which I doubted judging from the hanging utensils and the overflowing grocery bags, or he was Felix Unger incarnate. What, I wondered, letting my fancy take me where my brain never would, would it be like living with someone who was not only prettier than I, but undoubtedly more talented, definitely neater, and probably a better cook.

Don't be taken in by charm and good looks, warned an inner voice. *Remember Bundy.*

Not a fair comparison, I responded.

Handsome devil, intelligent, charming, the voice went on implacably.

Granted. But—

A psychopath. A killer without conscience.

So what are you saying? That Jonathan's the killer?

All I'm saying is be careful. Your job is to protect Meg and to find out what the hell this is about, not to start fantasizing about the first stud who comes along, no matter how much he reminds you of Robert Redford.

I was closing the refrigerator when my snoop-control mechanism went out of whack. What, I wondered, was our enigmatic host planning for dinner? Poison mushrooms, perhaps? A crumpled bag on the bottom shelf contained packages of mussels, little-neck clams, and plump pink succulent-looking shrimp. Normally, I lose my appetite when I'm stressed out, but the sight of those fresh crustaceans made my mouth water. I chose not to examine the package I noticed in the sink, sure I could guess at its contents. It was shaped like one of those plastic containers they give you in take-out restaurants, but it was much larger and as I peered at it, it moved. Lobster, I surmised, a favorite of mine so long as I don't have to do the boiling. Next to it was a metal utensil that looked unlike any cooking utensil I've ever used. I picked it up. It seemed to be a small forceps. Maybe Jonathan needed it to handle the lobster, although I couldn't imagine his being squeamish.

About to close the refrigerator door, I noticed that the butter compartment was taped shut with a bright yellow tape that reminded me of the crime-scene tape I'd crawled under less than an hour before. *"Keep out,"* it seemed to say. Unable to resist a no-trespass sign, I lifted the tape and opened the panel. Four vials and four syringes. I was mystified. Was Jonathan an addict? He displayed none of the symptoms. Maybe he was diabetic, but the contents of the vials didn't look like insulin, which I thought was clear. He wasn't a medical doctor. He was an EMT, though. Hadn't he said so when he was bandaging Meg's head? Were EMTs licensed to give shots? I didn't think so. I peered at the group of vials more closely. Each contained a strange-looking viscous black fluid.

"Carrie? What's happened to you?" Meg's voice.

Hearing footsteps, I quickly replaced the tape and shut the door. Jonathan's figure materialized in the doorway. The appraising look he cast my way made my palms sweat. I grabbed for the paper towel and wiped them dry.

"Can I help you find something?" he inquired pleasantly enough.

"Oh, no. I was just cleaning up." I gave a swipe at the counter with the towel and dropped it into the garbage. "Wanted to make sure I left the kitchen the way I found it." I forced a smile. "You either have an excellent cleaning woman, or you're the neatest man I've ever met."

I thought his answering smile matched mine for insincerity, but maybe it was my guilty conscience sticking it to me again. "I'm afraid it's the latter. I don't have a cleaning woman. Annoys the hell out of me, having strangers poking around in my things."

I picked up my drink and sidled past him. "I don't have a cleaning woman either. But only because I can't afford one."

"Can't afford what?" Meg asked, as I plopped myself down onto the couch beside her.

"A cleaning woman."

"Why in God's name are you talking about cleaning women?"

"It came up."

"I was telling Carrie that I don't have one because I value my privacy," Jonathan said pointedly. "But I agree. We have much more important things to discuss." His face grew serious as he settled his gaze on me. "What made you believe those men this afternoon were after you?"

"They came right for us. Followed us into the cemetery."

"Isn't it possible they were there for another reason? Maybe they were meeting someone."

"They started to run as soon as they saw us," Meg said.

"Straight *at* us," I interjected. "And who has meetings in a cemetery?"

"Did either of them look familiar?"

"The tall one reminded me of someone. Something about the way he moved . . ."

"Can you think who?"

"I can't place him." I turned to Meg. "Did he look familiar to you?"

"No. He had his hat pulled down, and when they started after us, everything blurred."

"What do you think they wanted?" Jonathan asked.

I sipped my drink, fixing my gaze on a painted fish dappled with reds and blues and greens who swam up to the glass and blew bubbles at me.

"Whoever killed Millie Larrabee was searching for something at the bed and breakfast," I heard Meg say. "Whatever it is, they must've thought we had it. Or that we know where it is."

Jonathan got up, walked over to the window, peered out, and then pulled the drapes closed. "Do you?" he asked.

Meg opened her mouth, but I got there first. "If we did, don't you think we'd have told the police?"

He turned around. "Why don't you let Meg answer?"

Well, well. This guy didn't trust me any more than I trusted him. I wondered why. What kind of threat could I possibly be to him? I gestured elaborately at Meg. "I beg your pardon. Go ahead, Meg."

Meg put her glass down on the table. "What's the matter with you two? We're not adversaries, are we?" She looked Jonathan straight in the eye. "I don't know what they're after, Jon."

He nodded, seeming to accept it from her. "Why'd you go out? I thought you said you were going to rest all day."

What made this guy think we had to answer to him? "We rested for a while," I replied sweetly. "It never occurred to us that taking a little walk would turn into a life-threatening situation."

"Why wouldn't it after what happened last night?

Don't you realize it could've been you lying on that floor?" He was the third person to point that out. As if I needed reminding every hour on the hour. Jonathan's fair skin turned dark red under the tan. It seems a trivial thing to have noted at that particular moment, but his eyes seemed to change color from deep blue to a startling blue-green. "For chrissake, two people've been killed already! Why would you deliberately expose yourselves to—"

"Jon," Meg interposed, expertly turning the attack aside. "Why didn't you tell me what that woman on the phone said about Christopher House?"

I focused my attention on one of those fish with a tail that looks like a head. It looked back at me with all four of its eyes. From under my lashes I glanced at Jonathan. His expression was impassive. "You'd had enough to deal with. I didn't think it was necessary to worry you about yet another call from some sicko." His eyes flashed to me, back to ice blue. "I'm sorry your *friend* wasn't able to keep her mouth shut."

I think I was correct in assuming he would never confide in me again.

"Maybe the call wasn't from some sicko," Meg protested. "I can't have you hiding things from me. What has no meaning for you might mean something important to me."

"Then I apologize. Does Christopher House mean anything special to you?"

I shot Meg a warning look.

"No." Meg hesitated. "But I might show up there on New Year's Eve."

"Maybe you'd like to join us," I purred, laying it on thick. "In that you already have a reservation, I mean." I smiled, enjoying my small victory.

"I see you've been checking up on me."

"Not you specifically. I saw your name on the New Year's Eve reservations list."

"And when was that?"

"I made it my business to have dinner at Christopher House last night."

Meg glanced at me, surprised, and I remembered I'd neglected to tell her where I'd met Banion. Jonathan didn't seem to notice her reaction.

"I've learned a lot the past couple of years, you know, Jonathan," I continued. "About never accepting things or people at face value. And like where there's smoke, there's fire."

"Well, how close you hold your own feet to the fire is your business, but maybe you ought to worry a little more about the possibility of Meg's getting burned in the process."

Whatever made me think this guy bore any resemblance to Robert Redford? He was definitely more of the Bundy type. I was suddenly feeling intensely hostile. He'd stung me, accusing me of recklessly endangering Meg, and I wanted to sting back, but I had no ammunition. So I said, à la my teenage daughter, "Oh, piss off," and flounced into the bedroom in high dudgeon.

UNLIKE MY TEENAGE DAUGHTER when she's in a flap, I did come out to eat. The aromas that wafted into the bedroom an hour later would have enticed a monk sworn to silence to sing for his supper.

The wound on Meg's head had been neatly re-bandaged and she and Jonathan were at the table deep in conversation when I sat down mumbling an apology for having behaved childishly.

"No, no. It was my fault. Sorry if I offended you, Carrie." Jonathan smiled at me over a paella fit for the gods. "After all, we both want to help Meg."

"Forget it. We're all a little touchy, and we've got other things to worry about."

"Yeah. Like how to keep you two alive."

"We'll stay put tomorrow," Meg assured him. "I promise."

"I'm wondering if you're safe here. You're okay while I'm home. I'm pretty good with a gun." He patted his jacket pocket, where I noticed a bulge. I wondered if he had a license to carry, but decided to leave that alone. "But," he continued, "I'm preparing for the race. I've got to leave by early afternoon."

I was thinking about his darkroom, thinking how I couldn't wait for him to leave so Meg could develop the film.

"Maybe I should call the police," he said, "and ask for a guard on the house. After last night I'm sure—"

"Not necessary," I interrupted. "I forgot to tell you. Ted's coming down tomorrow. He should be here by late afternoon."

"Ted?"

"Carrie's on-again, off-again significant other," Meg replied. "He's a cop, and for the moment"—she shot me an amused look—"apparently he's on-again."

"A cop. No shit." He regarded me quizzically over the top of his sangria glass. "Who'd've thought it?"

"What?"

"You and the law."

I wondered if I was being insulted. Maybe he'd

meant me and anybody at all. I speared a clam, chewed, and swallowed. "He's homicide," I dropped casually.

"Well, that's certainly convenient for you," he replied. And with serving spoon poised, he inquired, "Anyone for more paella?"

W E STASHED THE ROLL of film under my pillow and went to bed early. Meg took a sleeping pill and slept as though she'd been clubbed, never moving a muscle all night. I slept fitfully, waking with the sheets all tangled two or three times while it was still dark, my dreams disturbing but elusive. I did come wide awake sometime around six, after a frighteningly vivid dream in which I was being chased through the cemetery by a huge red crustacean with pincer claws. That's when it occurred to me that although there had been chicken and shrimp and clams and mussels and sausage in the paella, there hadn't been any lobster.

T UESDAY MORNING DAWNED BRIGHT and cool—cool being somewhere in the mid-seventies. I opened the window when I saw the palm trees swaying and felt a comforting breeze on my face. Looking up at a powder blue sky peppered with puff clouds and crying seabirds, I thought how sad it was that a place so beautiful would probably forever be associated with death in my mind.

As I showered and dressed, I began to map out the day. Meg had promised Jonathan to stay put, but I hadn't. The swelling in my ankle seemed to have completely disappeared and with it any remaining discomfort.

Before anything I wanted to check in with the kids. Young as they are, I was certain they would have been able to shake off their concern about Meg enough to enjoy the skiing, but I knew they were worried and would want an update on the situation here. Not that I had much to tell them. I certainly wasn't about to mention the second murder, or the little tidbit that their mother was the one who found the body. For the second time in a year yet. I didn't want to think about what Rich would make of that. He might decide I was an unfit mother and drag me back to court. The incident in the cemetery was hardly an appropriate topic of conversation either. I could go on about the scenery, I thought, describe the boats and the magnificent view from the pier, but I nixed the idea because it would bring to mind Pete and the way he had died. I sighed as I pulled on my jeans, deciding to put the call off till after breakfast.

As I struggled with hair gone frizzy from the humidity, I thought about Pete. The people he'd been hanging out with when Kev was still in Danbury had to be sources of information. I needed to go back down to the pier and pump some of the other racers.

More and more, it was becoming clear that trouble followed Pete like rats followed the Pied Piper. He attracted it, according to Meg, because he was always after the quick buck and because he was willing to do whatever it took to get it. Why had Kev refused to see his brother's failings? Would Pete be alive today if Kev had recognized who he was and refused to go along with his scheme?

God knows, I myself had certainly been guilty of

selective blindness, but relationships between husband and wife contain so many other elements. Sex, for one.

Sex. Pete had been an attractive man, a sexy man. He'd even come on to Meg, betraying Kev still again. *I'll bet there's a woman,* I thought suddenly. *A woman who knows something.* Guys like Pete always have one or more women on the string. And guys like Pete brag about their exploits to their women. *Cherchez la femme.* There was a place to begin. I decided that as soon as Meg had developed the film—provided what was on it didn't send us straight to the cops—I was going down to the marina to *cherche* Pete's woman.

I was dying to bounce my thoughts off someone. Then I remembered who was on his way down here and smiled at myself in the bathroom mirror. My favorite puzzle-solver would be here in a few hours. Too bad no matter what I did with my hair, I continued to look as if some beauty-school trainee had given me the first permanent of his or her career. A little selective blindness on Ted's part would be welcome.

"Almost eight-thirty, sleepyhead," I called out to Meg as I passed our bedroom on my way to the kitchen. "The bathroom's all yours."

The coffeepot was perking merrily away and there were muffins, croissants, and various condiments set out on the table. Whatever else I might have thought about Jonathan, I couldn't fault him as a host. I really should have been trying harder to get along with him. The old adage about catching a fly with honey rather than vinegar still applied. I wondered where he was as I poured myself a cup of coffee and buttered a blueberry muffin. Maybe he would join me for breakfast.

Mug in one hand and half a muffin in the other, I

crossed through the living room, being careful not to drop any crumbs. I called out, "Jonathan?"

No answer. I called again. "Jonathan, you in there?" I heard the sound of a chair scraping the floor coming from his bedroom, and I walked down the hall, pausing in the doorway. Jonathan was sitting in his desk chair, bent forward over the aquarium in the corner, totally absorbed in observing something on the floor of the tank.

"Would you like to join me for a cup of coffee?" I asked.

He jumped as though I'd shouted obscenities in his ear. "Jesus Christ, Carrie, do you always creep up on people like that?"

"Sorry." I tried not to appear miffed. "I did call you from the living room."

"Didn't hear you," he said, placing a cover on the aquarium and locking it in place. He didn't seem interested in conversation or coffee. Swiveling his chair around, he began typing furiously.

I stepped uninvited into the room, moving closer to the tank. The odd-looking thing, which certainly hadn't been in there yesterday, was about four inches long, with a brilliantly colored, conically shaped, intricately patterned shell. It was waving a wormlike projection in front of it as it inched its way forward. I watched as the projection speared a piece of floating debris and reeled it in. Matt has quite an extensive collection of seashells, but I'd never seen anything like this.

"What is that?" I asked, thinking I'd endear myself to my host by displaying an interest in his hobby. "Mattie would love one of those shells in his collection. Where'd you find it?"

"Not around here."

I moved closer. "It looks kind of like a snail."

"It is." His laugh was without mirth. "But I wouldn't make escargot out of it."

Foolish me, I kept trying. "Why don't you keep it in the big aquarium? Aren't snails bottom-eaters, good for keeping the tanks clean?"

"Not this species." He hit the SAVE button on the computer, shut it down, pushed his chair back, and got to his feet, ushering me firmly out of the room. "Is Meg awake?"

"Still sleeping when I got up. Took a pill last night."

"Good. She needed the rest."

Passing through the living room, he stopped to sprinkle fish food into some of the tanks. Snowy glowered at me from his underwater lair, while I swallowed the rest of my muffin and attempted to keep the conversation going. "Are there many different species of snail?"

"Yes. Of course, we're killing them off like we kill off everything that has the potential to benefit humanity."

"Other than eating them with lots of garlic, I never think of snails as benefiting humanity."

"That just shows how uninformed you are."

Okay, no warm fuzzies here. I wandered back into the kitchen and poured myself another cup of coffee. I was surprised to see my hand shaking. So the man didn't like me. So what? Not everybody likes everybody. I could accept that. So why did I feel like grinding muffin crumbs into his sparkling white tile floor? I actually reached for one before I got control of myself and decided to look for fuzzies elsewhere. I picked up the phone, punched in my credit-card number, and dialed the condo in Park City.

Rich answered, sounding like I'd awakened him. "Hullo."

"Hi," I said brightly. "It's me."

Grumpy. Not bright. No fuzzies. "Yeah, I know."

"Uh . . . can I speak to the kids?"

"For chrissake, Carrie, they're sleeping. It's six-fuck-ing-thirty here!"

I glanced at my watch. "Oh, God, I'm sorry. I forgot the time difference."

"I'll say."

Well, so long as he was up . . . "How's everything going?"

"Fine."

"Uh-huh. That's good. Kids enjoying the skiing?"

"Yeah, loving it."

I waited for him to ask about Meg. Difficult to believe that the children hadn't mentioned what had happened.

"I suppose they told you where I am and why."

"Yeah. How's Meg?"

Better late than never. "Having a rough time. You can imagine."

"Yeah."

Long pause.

"Well, go back to sleep. I'll call again in a couple of hours."

"The kids've got lessons at nine, and they're skiing with a group all day. Call tonight."

"You're . . . uh . . . not going with them?"

"They're okay. They like the group. It's all kids. Suz and I are taking a little break today."

I heard a giggle in the background, then a squeal, but refused to allow my imagination to dwell on the particulars.

"When're you going home?" he asked.

"Don't worry, I'll be there by the time you get back."

The pause on the other end of the line stretched uncomfortably long.

"Well," I said finally, "I guess—"

"Wait. I was thinking I might send them home on Saturday. Give myself a couple of free days to"—he caught himself—"have a couple of days to relax before getting back to the old grind."

So being a full-time daddy was wearing thin already. "You've been relaxing all week, Rich. I'm afraid you're going to have to tell *Suz* that these are your children and you're not going to cut their vacation short because they're cramping your style. Or hers."

"Christ, you've got a dirty mind."

"But right on, I'm sure. Anyway, there's no way I can get back till Monday."

Iceman. "Fine."

"Please tell Allie and Matt I called and I'll talk to them tonight."

"Right."

Not "Take care. Hope everything goes all right. Let me know." It bugged me that it still hurt.

"Bye," I said.

"Bye," he replied.

I hung up and put my head down on the table. For just a minute those old terrible feelings of isolation and loneliness swept over me. A sympathetic hand dropped onto my shoulder. I looked up. Jonathan was smiling down at me as though he hadn't just insinuated I was too dumb to live.

"I have a Jacuzzi out back," he said. "What do you say we put on suits and let it massage our cares away?"

And they accuse women of having mood swings.

J ONATHAN LEFT SHORTLY AFTER noon, with a warning to us about the dire consequences of our venturing forth without a regiment of marines to guard us. As soon as the door closed behind him and I heard the lock click into place, I grabbed the film from under my pillow and made for his darkroom, calling out to Meg to follow me.

Somewhat reluctantly, she did. "It seems so slimy, invading his privacy the minute his back is turned," she muttered as we walked down the hallway to his room.

"Oh, for God's sake, Meg, we're not stealing anything."

"I know, I know. Give me the film."

I handed it to her and reached for the door handle. The knob turned, but the door refused to budge. I pushed and shoved, hoping that somehow, unnoticed by us, the humidity had crept into the house and swelled the wood, making the door stick. I wanted to huff and puff and blow the damned thing in. "Why would he suddenly decide to lock his door?"

"He told us how he felt about people poking through his things," Meg said flatly. "Give it up."

"It wasn't locked yesterday. What's changed?"

"I don't know, but unless you're an expert lock-picker, stop wasting your energy."

"All right," I said when we were back in our room. "We go to Plan B. You stay here. I'll take the film over to one of those one-hour camera stores. There must be—"

"Too dangerous. You might be followed."

"I'll be okay. No one's after *me*."

"You think those guys yesterday didn't know we were together? Either both of us go or neither goes."

I gave in, deep-sixing for the time being my plan to go down to the pier. "Plan C, then. We'll wait for Ted and—"

"He'll turn it over to Springer and Hanover."

"So what? We're all—"

"On the same side? Maybe. I want to see what's on this film before the police get their hands on it."

What was Meg afraid of? I dreaded asking, so I didn't. "What do you suggest then?"

"Let me think."

The small room wasn't designed for pacing. Certainly not for two people pacing. On the second go-round, after a near collision between the twin beds, we moved to the living room. The sight of Marineland brought to mind the creature in Jonathan's room. I walked up and down that extraordinary glass wall, studying its inhabitants, looking for a similar kind of patterned shell. "Maybe it was the snail," I murmured.

"Excuse me?"

"The reason he locked his door. Maybe he didn't want us inspecting the latest acquisition."

"Why not, for God's sake?" She gestured toward the wall-to-wall sea life. "He's like a proud daddy with these."

"That's what's intriguing. Why isn't that thing in here with the rest of them?"

"Maybe it eats little fish."

"So do some of the bigger fish, and God knows what Snowy there eats," I said. The eel eyed me malevolently. "Probably us if he could get at us. The point is, Jonathan keeps the predators separate. But he keeps them in here. Not isolated in another room."

"Well, whatever his reason, it's obvious I can't use the darkroom unless we tell him why I want to."

"There may be another way." I sat down next to her on the couch.

"Yeah, go on."

Taking a deep breath, I plunged ahead. "There's something I need to tell you about Sy Banion."

She rolled her eyes. "Oh, please, not him again."

"He's FBI, Meg."

"*What?*"

"I had to swear not to tell you for your own safety and Kev's. They believe Kev's innocent and that he's alive and hiding from the mob."

I wasn't prepared for her reaction—the look of incredulity mixed with fury spreading over her face. Involuntarily, I slid a few inches away, but my thighs were suddenly damp with perspiration and stuck to the fabric.

"You had information that the FBI is involved, that they believe Kev is alive and *innocent*, and you didn't tell me?" She rose, eyes blazing, a flame-haired virago towering over me. I struggled to my feet and backed away. Meg's been taking classes in tae kwon do.

"I couldn't," I pleaded from my disadvantageous position two feet away and five inches below her. "Banion said if his cover got blown, you'd be—"

"That was no excuse to keep this from me! Kev is *my* husband. You had no right—"

"I was warned not to tell Ted or Springer either. Banion says the police wouldn't be able to protect either one of you if they found him first." I blurted out the whole story then, everything Banion had told me about Pete's using Mafia money and getting pulled into drug-running, about Kev's finding out and trying to renegotiate, and how the plan was that they were both supposed to have been killed in the boating accident.

"How do they know all that?"

I realized I hadn't asked. I dredged up memories from *Untouchables* reruns. "I suppose they have informants or people undercover."

"How did the mob kill Pete?"

"They think poison, like Hanover said. Something that didn't kick in right away. They're waiting for the results of the tissue analysis. And he said the motorcycle that was painted Kev's colors and almost ran us down was supposed to be a warning to you to quit asking questions."

She was silent for what seemed like an eternity. I watched as she moved away from me as if *I* had become untouchable. She walked over to the aquarium and pressed her forehead up against the cold glass. A spotted fish with a head that looked like a horse swam to the surface and looked her straight in the eye as if to say, "Ya can't trust anyone but your horse, kid."

When she turned to me, her voice was glacial. "How do you know Banion's who he says he is?"

"Everything he said made sense, Meg. And I saw his credentials. He told me to call FBI headquarters to verify."

"Did you?"

"With everything that's happened, I haven't had a chance. We can call now if you want."

We walked into the kitchen and Meg handed me the phone. I called information and asked for the number for Miami FBI headquarters.

"FBI," came a voice over the line after I'd pressed in the number. "How may I direct your call?"

"I'd like to speak with Director Crenshaw, please."

A pause, then a deep male voice said, "Crenshaw."

I held the phone so Meg could hear. "I'd like to get in touch with one of your agents, please. A Mr. Simon Banion?"

"Banion's in the field. Can I help you or do you want his voice mail?"

"His voice mail, please."

There was another pause, then Simon's voice. "This is Special Agent Simon Banion. Please leave your name and number, and your call will be returned."

"It's definitely him," I said to Meg.

"I still don't understand why he would have wanted you to know about this, though."

"I was supposed to keep you out of harm's way till Sunday, and then get you to Pier House to watch the races."

"Why?"

"In the hope Kev would see you and make contact."

"Bait, you mean. A worm on a fishhook."

"We'd be with Banion. You'd both have been protected," I mumbled with more assurance than I felt.

"I trust you'll remember to engrave that on our tombstones when you bury us next to Pearl. You intend to tell all this to Ted when he gets down here?"

"Banion said things were moving faster than he'd expected, so he'd be coming over, probably today, to explain the whole thing to you. I'd hoped by the time Ted got here it'd all be out in the open. You know what a lousy liar I am. I'd never've been—"

"Please. You don't give yourself enough credit."

I crossed over to where she stood, touched her arm, silently asking forgiveness. She turned away.

"I had no choice, Meg. I didn't want anything to

happen to you. That's why I didn't want you to come with me today if I went out."

"I'm a big girl. I'll make my own decisions." She picked up the key off the coffee table and stuffed the film down her bra.

"Where are you going?"

"Research. Now that I know I'm not the only one who's sure Kevin's alive, I'm going to find out what they want with him."

"Who? The mob?" She'd flipped out. I trailed her into the kitchen to the back door. "You're going to beard the lion in his den, so to speak?"

"You got it."

"Who're you going to be looking for, Brando or Pacino?"

Pulling the curtains on the door slightly apart, she peered out. "I'm going down to the marina. Somebody there must know who runs the show here."

"Well, if that's what you want to do, I can save you shoe leather. Go sit on the front porch and let them come and get you. Or better yet, why don't you save them the trouble of killing you? We'll go down to Fury Dock and you can jump off."

She whirled on me. "How much longer do you think I can sit here doing nothing? You've just told me that Kev was supposed to die along with Pete, that there's a mob contract out on him. And that your Mr. Banion and the entire FBI haven't been able to do zilch about any of it. Well, something tells me the mob's tentacles reach farther than the FBI's. The longer this goes on, the closer they're going to get to Kev. He can't hide out forever. So I'll get down on my hands and knees and beg this Mafia don to take his money—if that's what he's after— in installments, and I'll work my fingers to the bone to pay him off. But what I won't do is let my husband die for something that selfish, worthless shit of a brother of his got him into. Now, you have a choice. You can come with me, or you can stay here and play peekaboo with Snowy."

I was saved from having to hit her over the head and tie her up by the ringing of the doorbell. It propelled us out the kitchen door as though the bell were a dynamite blast. With our backs pressed up against the shingles, we started in the direction of the front porch, inching our way through the lush greenery hugging the house.

"Maybe it's Simon," I whispered, grabbing Meg's shirt.

"More likely it's those goons we ran into yesterday," Meg whispered back.

"I thought you wanted to talk to them."

"Not them. The boss. Whoever they're working for."

A jutting branch from a bush jabbed itself into my calf, and I suppressed a yelp of pain. "Well, in case you haven't noticed, we're headed in the wrong direction," I whispered hoarsely. "Why are we—"

"I want to see what they look like."

Forget about diverting Meg when she's made up her mind. By the time we'd made our stealthy way around the side of the house to where we could see the porch, it was empty. No car was parked in front of the house. I glanced down the street, but saw no one lurking behind the sturdy trunks of the tall royal palms or the convoluted roots of the lone banyon.

"Well, whoever it was, he's gone," I said, in my relief not bothering to lower my voice.

"Wrong," hissed a voice in my ear, and two strong arms pinned my arms to my sides.

I let out a shriek, as every hair on my head unfrizzed

and stood straight up. Then the arms loosened and I twisted around, prepared to go for the eyes. For one brief second words failed me. Except for one. "Shit!" When air returned to my lungs, I managed to croak, "Damn you, Ted Brodsky. You scared me half to death! Don't you ever sneak up on me like that again!"

"Next time *you* want to sneak up on someone," he said grinning, "watch your flank." He stepped back, and his brows drew together as his gaze settled on Meg. My anger melted like ice cream on a hot day as I watched him walk over to her and enfold her in a warm embrace. "Sorry if I scared you, Meg. How're you doin'?"

She hugged him back, making an effort to smile. "Been a lot better, but I'm happy to see you."

I allowed myself a minute to recover my composure and to deal with my reaction—part overwhelming relief, part heart-fluttering excitement. The obvious was that Meg and I finally had an ally. What was more threatening to my sense of independence was that just seeing Ted's face made me want to grin like an idiot and rub up against him like my cats do to me when I've been away all day. I decided it was hormonal. I was definitely going to have to do something about my sex life. He was wearing chinos, sneakers, and a short-sleeved blue sport shirt, wrinkled now, open at the neck. I focused on his face, on how tired he looked, the little lines around his eyes more pronounced than usual. I guessed he'd taken an early flight into Miami, probably hadn't had his usual five hours. "You look tired," I said with just the right mix of concern and friendliness.

He replied in kind with an amused glint in his eye. "May I say the same to you."

"She'll sleep better now that you're here," Meg said.

"I hope not," he teased.

"You're out of luck, fella. No hotels. You're going to have to bunk with Springer." I turned to Meg. "Or do you think he's more Hanover's type?"

"You two work it out. I have places to go, people to see. I'll catch up with you later."

"Wait a minute," I said quickly. "We're coming with you."

"Where're we off to?" Ted asked, falling into step beside us.

"The boatyard. Meg wants to talk to"—I caught her warning look—"some of the guys on the race teams."

"Can we stop for a bite on the way? I'm starving. The breakfast on the plane filled about one toe."

"They have food stands coming out the kazoo down there. You'll think you're at the U.N. You can sample specialties from every country in the world."

"I really think I'm better off going alone," Meg said. "The people I want to talk to may not appreciate an entourage."

In 'bad cop' guttural, Ted grunted, "Lady, me and my partner here, we make people talk for a livin'."

"He's the marines, our safe-conduct pass," I whispered into Meg's ear. "After yesterday we may need him."

Ted caught the last sentence. "What about yesterday?"

"I'll tell you about it after you've filled your face. You'll be in a better mood."

He turned appraising eyes on me, but refrained from saying anything. We walked for quite a way in silence, past the little Victorian houses that line Southard Street, past the gaily decorated tourist shops on Duval, making our way through crowds of sun and sea-worshipers toward the shimmering blue froth-capped water in the distance. Despite the seriousness of our situation, I could see Ted enjoying the atmosphere. I wondered when he'd last taken a vacation. For that matter, I couldn't remember the last time I had.

"By the way, Meg," Ted said. "Have you ever met either of Pete's ex-wives?"

"I knew Kate. I never met Maxie, the first one."

"What do you know about her?"

"Very little. Kev said she was quite beautiful."

"It might be worthwhile talking to her. You know where she's living now?"

"If Pete knew, he never said. She caught Pete and Kate in her bed. Somehow I don't think she'd be interested in helping find his killers."

Ted glanced at me as we turned onto Caroline Street, caught me looking nervously over my shoulder. "What's the matter with you?"

"Nothing. I'm admiring the scenery. Isn't it gorgeous here?"

"Paradise."

"Paradise lost," said Meg.

Ted stopped walking. "Okay, I can listen on an empty stomach. I want to know who you thought I was back there."

So I brought him up to date. I left out that we'd gone to the B&B specifically to get the film, figuring it was a small omission and I'd make a few much-needed points with Meg by keeping that between us for now. In the telling, the saga of the goons in the cemetery lost some of the terror we'd felt and took on drama and even humor. I was embellishing the part about Pearl's marker when Ted, who wasn't smiling at my wit, interrupted.

"Hold it. Are you telling me you were being chased

by a couple of armed thugs with murder on their minds and Springer hasn't put a guard on you?"

"We haven't had a chance yet to—"

He looked at me in disbelief. "You didn't tell him."

"There've been things our Carrie hasn't seen fit to tell *me* until today," Meg said, making it clear she was still ticked off and so far as she was concerned, I could stew in my own goulash.

Fortunately, just then we arrived at the entranceway to the boat area. Meg showed her pass, Ted flashed his badge, and I smiled. "We're together," I announced loftily, gesturing at Ted. Police power. The guard waved us on.

"Man, oh, man, 'if I were a rich man,' " Ted breathed in awe as he surveyed the marina, where luxury high-performance boats, speedboats, cruisers, and sailboats—one more eye-catching than the next—dotted the horizon. We wound our way through the trailers and boats in the parking area, feeling a bit like Gulliver's Lilliputians. I caught Ted touching one or two sleek hulls as we passed. Just beyond the lot our senses were assaulted by the sounds and smells of the food stalls. Ted stopped at a booth displaying a large blue and white banner reading, A TOUCH OF GREECE. THE BEST SOUVLAKIS, GYROS, AND KABOBS THIS SIDE OF ATHENS.

"I'm going down to the dock," Meg said.

"Why don't you wait and let Ted—"

"Meet me there."

And before I could stop her, she'd disappeared into the jostling crowds. I saw a figure on the dock give a friendly wave as she approached.

Munching on a massive gyro that dripped milky juices, Ted joined me. "I have a feeling I am going to need sustenance to listen to the rest of this story."

He was going to need more than a gyro. I decided to see how chemistry would work. "Lose the onions. I haven't properly welcomed you yet."

Promptly he opened the roll, fished out the offenders, and dropped them into a nearby trash container.

"I'm really glad you're here," I whispered.

He caught me to him. "I'm really glad to hear it. You had me wondering."

Taking his face in my hands, I kissed him—a long, satisfying kiss. When I opened my eyes, I saw a couple of teenage girls watching us and giggling. I sighed and pulled away. "Your gyro's getting cold."

He grinned. "How many starving men would sacrifice a gyro for a kiss from you?"

"When I tell you what I've been doing, you may opt for the gyro."

"Uh-oh." He placed his Coke by his feet and sat on one of the plastic benches. "Hit me."

I stayed on my feet so I could keep Meg in view and told him about my going to Christopher House. This drew frown lines between his brows but no comment because, before he could swallow, I was into my meeting with Sy Banion. "When I read about this guy Kristal, gunning down Diamantopoulos, I remembered what Banion told me on the plane. It all began to come together. Because the guy who hired Kristal had mob connections."

"You're talking about Alex Diamantopoulos, the powerboat mogul? What's that got to do with this?"

"He was murdered by the mob over a bad business deal."

Ted was staring at an array of nautical banners strung on a rope across from us, but I could tell he wasn't seeing them. His thoughts were turned inward. I could almost see him sorting the puzzle pieces in his head.

"I remember the case. There are people who believe Diamantopoulos was hit by the mob for other reasons and it wasn't Kristal who did it," he said after a minute.

"Didn't Kristal confess?"

"He made a deal. He was a three time loser. What's bothering me is that since Diamantopoulos' murder, the mob has been less involved in using these powerboats for drug-running. It was kind of the end of an era."

"But if Pete owed them money, it was a way of collecting."

"Ummm . . . yeah, but the wasting of the landlady doesn't fit. Not their style. Besides, if Pete had already invested the money in the business, he wouldn't have it, would he? So what is it they think Meg and Kevin are hiding?"

Following his train of thought, I slapped my head. It was so obvious, I don't know why it hadn't occurred to me. "Drugs! Pete must have picked up drugs and didn't turn them over. Maybe Kev destroyed them, or maybe Pete needed money and sold the stuff on the street. That must be why they're after Kev."

Ted nodded. "One possibility."

"They must think Kev or Pete told Meg where the stuff is. That'd be why Banion wants her to stay out of sight till the races on Sunday."

"I'd like to talk to this guy. Makes no sense for him not to be working with the locals on this."

"If you met Hanover you'd understand. Anyway, you'll have your chance. He'll be coming to Jonathan's today to talk to Meg."

"Good."

A pelican perched on one leg on a stanchion near us,

his beady eyes focused on the clear water. Suddenly he spotted his prey and, in one swift motion, swooped down and had the struggling fish in its beak. The sight suddenly made my stomach go queasy. "Ugh! Imagine being eaten alive."

Ted followed my gaze. "Nature's way. Bottom of the food chain."

"Pete thought he could swim with the sharks," I murmured. "But they ate him alive."

"That is one off-the-mark analogy. Pete was not an innocent fish just swimming along minding his own business."

"Whatever he was, he was way out of his league," I said unhappily.

"Tell me about Meg and Pete."

"What do you mean?"

"You said she didn't like him."

"What would you expect after Kev went to jail for something Pete did, and then Pete never even went to see him? Besides, he came on to her while Kev was still in Danbury."

"She told you he ran with a fast crowd."

"Yeah, but that wasn't what bothered Meg. She thought he was doing what he needed to do to sell boats."

"But she didn't want Kevin to be in business with him."

"Not after what had happened the last time. Who could blame her?"

Ted got up and went over to the trash can, crushed the cup, and tossed it and the remains of his gyro down the slot. "I wonder, though, if she knew about the drug-running, how far she would have gone to stop him."

Styrofoam makes noise when you crush it. I must have heard wrong. "What?"

"Didn't you tell me Meg was at Fury Dock the day of the accident?"

"Yes, but she left before it happened. What are you . . ."

"Let's go down to the pier. Meg and I need to talk."

"What did you just say?"

"I was thinking aloud."

"Talk about off the mark. If you think Meg could in any way be—"

"Hey, hey, don't put words in my mouth."

"The words already came out of your mouth." I planted myself firmly in his path. "Kev was on that boat too."

"I know."

"So how can you—"

He sighed. "Carrie, I'm a cop. I look at every possibility, no matter how remote or how farfetched it may seem to other people."

"Oh, right. I certainly remember that about you."

His eyes twinkled. "But I'm fair. I'm more than happy to admit when I'm wrong."

He reached for me again, but I twisted away. "I am not feeling very affectionate."

We were almost at the pier. I'd taken my eyes off Meg, but I looked up in time to see a boat with a man and a woman on deck pulling away. I almost fell as I scrambled down the rocky terrain. If Ted hadn't grabbed me, I'd have sprawled flat on my face on the loose gravel.

"Meg," I shouted, recovering my balance and jerking loose from his grasp. "Where're you going?"

But the noise of the engines drowned out my voice. Through the spray I saw her, tall, long-legged, in T-shirt and cutoffs, wearing a life jacket and a shiny orange helmet.

"Meg!" I yelled again, jumping up and down and waving my arms frantically. "Ted," I screamed. "Call somebody! Call the Coast Guard! We've got to stop them!"

"Jesus God, Carrie, you'll have Security all over us. I'm right here. What are you yelling about?"

I turned around. Meg was sitting on a pile of life jackets, her knees drawn up to her chin, looking at me as though I'd suddenly gone beserk. Relief washed over me. "I . . . I thought you were on that boat. I thought you were going to . . . I saw a woman with a helmet—"

"Why would I get on Stu Kellerman's boat? I just met the man and he had nothing to tell me."

I sank down on a life jacket next to her, took her hand as though to anchor her. "He's one of Banion's people."

"For God's sake, why didn't you let me know? I would have asked him—"

"I forgot. But it's better you didn't say anything."

"Who was the woman with him?" Ted asked.

"Francine Somebody."

"That's Banion's girlfriend. Or maybe she isn't. I'll bet she's an agent too."

Ted held out his hand to Meg. "There's one way to get the answers, and I think it's time we did. Why don't we head back and Carrie can give her friend a call?"

Meg got to her feet, brushing dirt off the seat of her shorts. "I'm finished here anyway."

I moved close to her and lowered my voice. "Did you talk to anyone who—"

Quickly, she cut me off. "A dead end," she whispered. "Nobody wants to admit they know anyone with mob connections."

I didn't believe her. I caught the expression that flashed over Ted's face, a dangerous mixture of annoyance and frustration. "You want to let me in on this conversation?"

Meg spoke before I could blow it. "I asked some of the guys to let me talk to anyone they can think of who Kev might contact if he needed help. If they come up with anything, they'll be in touch."

True as far as it went, and Meg didn't give Ted the opportunity to worm anything else out of her. She marched determinedly up the slope ahead of us.

Ted watched her for a minute, then turned to me. "Where'd you think she was going on that boat, Carrie?"

I avoided his gaze. "I don't know."

"You were in a panic. Who was she going to meet?"

"Really, I was just worried because—"

"If you're going to lie, at least learn to look me in the eye." Ted's voice was harsh. Only once before could I remember him taking that tone with me—when I'd broken into an apartment and discovered a dead body.

I looked him in the eye. "I can't tell you."

"Goddamm it, I came down here to help. Don't tie my hands. You just talked about a possible Mafia connection. Don't tell me Meg's seriously considering talking to someone connected to the mob?"

"I'm not telling you that." Hell, I was *deliberately* not telling him that. I started to sweat, and it wasn't the sun. It wasn't that I disagreed with Ted. What Meg was planning was crazy, but maybe it was just crazy enough to work, and if I did something to jeopardize it and something subsequently happened to Kevin, she'd never forgive me, whether or not it was related to my big mouth.

Ted read me like a book, saw that I was in a quandary, and—damn him—played his ace.

"I don't suppose it's occurred to you that by your misguided collusion in this, you may be instrumental in your friend's walking into a situation she's totally unequipped to deal with."

I swallowed, trying to work up some saliva. "Meg's tough. She can handle herself," I mumbled.

He glared at me. "That's the biggest load of bullshit I've ever heard out of your mouth. Christ almighty, Carrie, these men are killers! Do you understand? Organized crime. The real thing. This is not a film where somehow we find ourselves sympathizing with a guy who's whacked thirty people. These people look on you and me *and Meg* like bugs to be exterminated if we get in their way. If Meg thinks she can appeal to some sense of decency, work out a deal to save Kevin, she's dreaming. And if you think you're doing her a favor by keeping your mouth shut—which is unusual for you, to start with—you'd better do some pretty hard rethinking."

He took off, leaving me standing there with my mouth open, definitely not shut. Until he caught up with Meg, we looked like a family of old-world Japanese wives—out of order to be sure, with Meg in the lead, Ted following, and me dragging up the rear.

Now everyone's pissed at me, I thought grumpily. *All I need is for those goons from yesterday to show up.* And taking my frustration out on the nearest inanimate object, I used my good foot to send a spray of pebbles flying toward a huge red boat trailer parked on the grass.

"Hey, you there! Lady in blue striped shirt . . ."

I paused, looking around. I couldn't tell where the voice was coming from, but I was the only one I could see wearing a blue striped shirt.

"You. Tha's right. I talkin' to you."

Adrenaline flowed as my eyes searched the area. Poised for flight, I half expected the owners of the black baseball caps to spring out from the leather-lined interior of a parked boat. Instead, almost as terrifying, like a rattler rising out of a snake charmer's basket, a large unshaven black man wearing a hot pink and green knit cap over dreadlocks rose from a pile of rags near the wheel of the trailer. He was barefoot, wearing dirty cut-off jeans and no shirt. The sign on his chest read, BLESSED ARE THEY WHO HELP THE HOMELESS HELP THEMSELVES. I glanced around for Meg and Ted. They were sitting on a bench, deep in conversation. At least, Ted's mouth was moving. Meg was silent, stubbornly staring at her feet. I figured I was safe enough. They were within hailing distance.

The man came so close I could smell a faint mixture of booze and cologne. I stepped back.

"I be sellin' clothes for food," he whined. "I don' be askin' for no charity." He grinned, displaying a mouthful of tobacco-stained teeth, reached up a bony hand, and pulled the knit cap off his head. "This all I got left and still be decent. I sell you this hat, knitted by me very own mother, for only one dollar."

"No, thank you," I muttered, casting around for an avenue of escape.

"Cost five in town."

"I thought your mother made it." *All these rich yuppies,* I thought morosely, *and this guy picks me for a touch.* The noisy crowds pushed past us, seeing but not seeing, oblivious to my plight. I could've called out to Ted, but I took the line of least resistance, stuck my hand in my pocket, and pulled out a dollar.

"Here," I said. "Now, go away."

"Take the hat," he insisted. "I no thief."

"I don't want it."

"Take it." There was menace in his tone. I grabbed the thing with my thumb and forefinger, skirted around him, and took off. I was breathless when I arrived at the bench.

"Never can find a cop when you need one," I grunted, dropping down beside Ted. I flipped the cap toward the trash container, missed, and watched it fall to the ground. I ignored the clunk it made as it struck the container.

"What's that?" Ted asked.

"Some wino started up with me. Wanted a handout. Intimidated me out of a buck."

Ted raised his eyebrows in mock horror. "So you stole the poor guy's hat? Man, you are one tough lady."

I don't know what Meg had said to him, but I was glad to see his anger toward me had dissipated. "I paid a dollar for that thing. You can have it for fifty cents."

"Ha. You're lucky I don't arrest you for littering." He got up, walked over to the trash can, picked up the cap, and was about to drop it down the slot, when suddenly he stopped and began turning it over in his hands.

"What're you doing?" I said. "Throw it away. God knows what's living in it."

"Where's the guy you got it from?"

"Right over there by the red . . ." I looked around for my tormentor. The pile of rags was where it had been, but the man had melted into the crowd.

"He had a buck in his pocket. Probably went for his fix."

Ted was holding the cap toward the sunlight, and I saw the rays bounce off something shiny.

"What is that?"

Ted came over and held the knit cap out so Meg and

I could both see it. "Either of you ever come across anything like this before?"

Pinned to the side of the cap was the object I'd heard hitting the trash bin. Our simultaneous gasp could have been orchestrated. We stared in stunned silence at the familiar powerboat-shaped, blue and silver enamel pin, on which you could clearly see a tiny jewel-handled miniature machete.

WE TOLD TED ABOUT the checked hat with the exact same pin on it that the police had found washed up on the beach.

"I know he's alive," Meg said, her face more animated than I'd seen it in days. "If you could get a fingerprint off it and it was Kev's, that'd be proof, wouldn't it?"

"Never get anything off the cap itself. Maybe off the pin though," Ted mused. "Carrie, see if anyone has a paper bag at one of the booths."

"I'll go." Meg was moving before I could stop her, and I let her go. There were things I wanted to ask Ted.

"Could they lift a print off the pin?"

"Possible, if it hasn't rubbed off. Too bad it's enameled."

"Does that make a difference?"

"Much easier to get a print off an unpainted metal surface. At least we know whose print we're looking for."

"But maybe Kev's never been—" I stopped, realizing I was talking about a man who'd done time. His fingerprints would be easily accessible.

"No way this guy you saw could've been Kevin in some sort of disguise, could it?" he asked.

"Ted, he was black."

"Oh. Describe him."

"Tall, maybe an inch or two shorter than you, but a broader build. He had dreadlocks, and . . . um . . . he was wearing cutoffs, no top, just a sign that said something about helping the homeless help themselves. Oh, and he had an accent, like from the islands."

"Pretty good. Make a detective out of you yet. Weight?"

"Oh, maybe . . . I don't know how to gauge men's weight. How much do you weight?"

"One sixty-five."

"Well, he was shorter, but more muscular. Maybe one seventy."

"Any distinguishing marks?"

"Didn't notice. I just wanted to get away from him." I thought hard, trying to bring something back. "He smelled—now that I think of it, he smelled like Rich when he's been drinking."

He grinned. "I'm sure Rich'd be thrilled with the comparison."

"It was the mixture of booze and cologne. The cologne smelled like that Chanel stuff Rich used to douse himself with on his evenings out. God, I should've know the business meetings were a fiction from that alone. *Pour Monsieur*, I think it was called."

"This guy who sleeps in a cardboard box was wearing Chanel cologne?"

"Well, I guess it couldn't have been."

"Unless the homeless thing was an act."

"You think he's a link to Kev?"

"I think he knows something. He picked you out of the crowd."

"Why me? Why not Meg?"

"Probably saw Meg with me. You were alone."

"But no one knew we'd be here today."

"It was a pretty safe bet you'd be here sometime this week. Guy's probably been watching for you."

I glanced around, my eyes searching the crowd. "Maybe we can find him."

"If I'm right he's long gone. I'm going to see you and Meg get back to Olsen's in one piece, and then I'm going to the station to take a look at the other pin."

I nodded. "What do you think—"

Ted placed a warning hand on my arm as Meg came running up, clutching a paper shopping bag. "Not so easy to find around here," she said breathlessly, holding it out to Ted. "Nobody bags anything."

Carefully, Ted dropped the cap into the bag. "Meg," he said, "I'm going to bring this over to the police lab and introduce myself to Springer. Do me a favor and stay in this afternoon. Don't expose yourself to danger. We might find out something from this that could help us locate Kevin. Can I have your word that you'll give me today at least to see what I can come up with?"

I flashed from one to the other. I couldn't believe Meg had admitted anything to Ted regarding her intentions, but she had to know he suspected something. Chances were she wouldn't hear from anyone today anyway. She must've been thinking that too, because she shrugged and nodded.

"Okay."

"Good," Ted said. "I didn't want to have to handcuff you to the furniture."

"If you play your cards right," I told Ted as we headed for the gate, "Jonathan might invite you to dinner. Among his other talents, he is one terrific cook."

"I can hardly wait to meet this paragon," he said dryly.

We walked swiftly and for the most part silently up Duval Street, then made a left onto Eaton, where the crowds of tourists began to thin.

"Tell me more about Banion," Ted said.

"I've only met him twice—once on the plane and the night we had dinner."

"How'd he approach you?"

"He noticed I was nervous, thought it was about flying, so he sat next to me and tried to get my mind off it."

"You realize he must have known who you were."

"Well, yeah, now that I think of it. I guess he planned the meeting."

"He ever show you his creds?"

"His what?"

"Credentials. He'd've had a small badge and—"

"And a card. Of course. He showed them to me in the restaurant. And Meg and I checked with his field office."

"Good. When we get home I want you to call him and arrange a meeting."

"He already said he's coming over."

"Set a time. I want to be there."

I smiled. "You don't like him because he's not working with the local cops. You guys and your interservice competitiveness."

"What I don't like is his dragging you into this."

"I was already in it."

"Tell me about the girlfriend."

"She's stunning. Clothes and jewelry to die for, a lot younger than he is, maybe twenty years." I caught Meg and Ted exchanging smiles. "Well," I muttered, "what these middle-aged fools refuse to recognize is that what the young women are attracted to is in their wallets, not their pants."

Ted grinned. "They know. They just don't give a damn."

Sheepishly, I joined in their laughter. "Well, like I said, maybe she's not really his girlfriend. Maybe she's part of his cover."

"Poor guy," Ted quipped. "Tough assignment."

"Poor you," I shot back. "No *undercovers* for you."

We were silent for the remainder of the walk to Jonathan's, but the wheels in our heads were whirring like window fans on high speed.

As we rounded the corner onto Angela, I was surprised to see the Jeep parked in the driveway. "Didn't Jonathan say he was going to be gone all day?" I asked Meg.

"It's almost four. He must've finished early."

I heard the printer humming as soon as we walked in the door. "He's in his room," I whispered to Ted. "C'mon. I want you to see the thing he's got in the small tank."

But Ted was staring, flabbergasted, at the wall-length marine reef aquarium. "Hooollly shit," he breathed.

"Impressive, huh?" I said.

"Astounding would be more like it."

"Come meet Snowy the Ravenous," I said, taking his hand. "The ancient Romans used to deck these eels out in jewels and feed them pushy cops."

"Don't listen to the woman. Snowy would never eat a cop. Too chewy. He likes tender meat."

I looked up and saw Jonathan's muscular frame in the doorway. "Hi," he said to Ted. "I'm Jonathan Olsen. You must be Carrie's friend."

"Ted Brodsky." Ted walked over to him, hand extended.

"Nice to meet you," Jonathan responded pleasantly. "Wish it could've been under happier circumstances."

Seeing them standing together—two extremely attractive males—there was no question which of the two most women would go for. Not me, though. I'd choose the lanky, craggy-faced one with the jagged scar on his shoulder. Badge of honor, result of eighteen years of service. My problem is, how many more badges will there be before he quits?

"That's quite an assemblage you've got here," said Craggy Face admiringly. "Must've taken you years to put it together."

"I've been collecting since I was a kid," Jonathan answered.

"Expensive hobby," Ted added. "Some of these specimens must be pretty rare."

"Come from all over the world," Jonathan said, beaming at the prospect of a fresh audience.

Before he could get started, I insinuated myself into the conversation. "I'm curious about that weird-looking snail you keep in the little tank in your room. Where does it come from?"

"The Phillipines," Jonathan replied. He turned back to Ted. "Let me show you a really rare specimen. . . ."

"Why do you keep it separate?"

"It's a research project."

"What kind of research?"

"Too complicated to explain." He walked to the other end of the room, making it explicitly clear the snail discussion was over. "Know anything about marine life, Ted?"

"About as much or as little as anybody who watches the Discovery Channel," Ted laughed. "I'm afraid it's not my area of expertise."

Jonathan was about to launch into an elaborate discourse on his favorite topic, but Ted forestalled him, leading the conversation in the direction he wanted.

"Carrie tells me you're also a diver, that you pulled Pete Reilly to shore."

"Yeah." Jon shook his head, his face suddenly somber. "First one I've ever lost."

"From what I've been told, no one could have saved him. I'd like to hear the circumstances from your perspective though."

I saw Meg blanch. "Jonathan," I said, "Meg looks as if she could use a pick-me-up. And so could I. Would you mind if we get something to drink while you and Ted talk?"

"No, no, go ahead. There's a pitcher of iced tea in the fridge. You want anything?" he asked Ted.

"Not right now. Carrie, why don't you go make your call?"

I nodded assent and followed Meg into the kitchen.

"Thanks," Meg said, sinking into a chair. "I absolutely could not have listened to it again."

"No reason why you should," I said. "But Ted'll pick up on any holes in Jonathan's story."

"Why do you keep implying there might be holes?"

"I'm just saying 'if.' If there are any. Ted's clever about finding discrepancies."

"Hell, I'm glad he doesn't suspect me."

I felt myself flush and turned away, busying myself putting ice in the glasses and pouring the tea. I knew Ted didn't seriously suspect Meg, but we both knew she'd protect Kevin with her life. If she was aware of anything she thought might implicate him, she'd keep it to herself. Women are such fools.

I passed the glass of tea to Meg, took a swallow of

mine, and reached for the phone. As I expected, I got Banion's answering machine and left a message that we were back at Jonathan Olsen's and would he please meet us here around eight this evening. I could hear the rumble of the men's voices as Ted and Jon talked, but I was suddenly so drained that I dropped down in a chair beside Meg's, forgoing any attempt at evesdropping.

A half hour later they appeared in the doorway. "Jonathan's going to drive me to the precinct," Ted said. "Promise you'll stay in."

"Word of honor."

"Meg?"

Meg didn't even open her eyes. "I swear. I'm too tired to go anywhere."

"I left a message for Sy Banion to meet us here tonight," I told them. "Around eight."

"We'll be back. Put the chain on the door after we leave."

I heard the door close and the lock turn, but I couldn't summon the energy to move. "You know," I said as I contemplated my haggard reflection in one of Jonathan's shiny frying pans, "if the mob doesn't kill us, the stress will."

"You're the biofeedback maven," Meg mumbled. "Do your thing."

I put my head down on my folded arms, closed my eyes, and made the effort, but I was fresh out of calmness and serenity. "There are some situations," I said, "that defy even my wizardry."

Within minutes exhaustion overtook me and I drifted off.

I am sitting in the aquarium, nestled in a bed of swaying ferns. Like a mermaid, I am breathing underwater. Around me, colorful fish and snails with brightly decorated shells waving magenta tube-

like projections form a dazzling kaleidoscope. I look up, and through an incandescent blue haze I see Meg standing above me snapping pictures. Suddenly, there's a shadow . . . huge, threatening. I open my mouth to cry out, and water rushes into my lungs. Gasping for air, desperate to warn Meg, I begin thrashing wildly, kicking at my glass prison . . .

And fell off the chair, landing on the hard white tile of Jonathan's kitchen floor. "Ouch!"

Meg jerked awake. "What's the matter? What happened?"

Embarrassed, I got to my feet, rubbing my hip. "I guess I dozed off. I was having this crazy dream that I was a mermaid inside the aquarium with all the fish, and you were taking pictures . . ." I stopped.

"Don't tell me. You fell off your rock."

"Never mind." I was already moving. "This is our chance. Get the film. Ten to one Jonathan forgot to lock his door."

"Ten to one you're wrong. He's the most organized man I've ever met."

JONATHAN'S DOOR STOOD WIDE open. I noticed that his computer monitor had been left on screen saver, two unheard of memory lapses for so meticulous a man. I wondered if Ted's arrival had rattled him.

Ignoring both the computer and the small aquarium with its solitary occupant, Meg made a beeline for the darkroom, fished the roll of film out of her bra, and closed the door behind her. "Remember," she called out. "Don't open the door after the red light goes on."

"Hey, I know that much," I called back, mildly insulted. I waited till the light beamed its warning, then wandered around the room, trying to get a handle on the personality of the man who lived here. Granted, Jonathan was excessively neat, so one wouldn't expect clutter, but everyone has some family or friends. Where were the pictures, the personal touches? A hunk like him with no girlfriends—or, another possibility, no boyfriends? If that were the case, maybe his interest in Meg was purely platonic. What did he read besides books pertaining to his profession? Finally, no more enlightened than when I came in, I sat in the chair by the computer, watching the snail as it waved its appendage like some kind of oversize antenna in front of it. I decided that, whatever Jonathan's sexual preference, it didn't dominate his life. He was a loner, one of those people so caught up in his work that he could relate only to things that swam or crawled.

I swiveled the chair in lazy circles, avoiding focusing on the monitor. It was an accident that my elbow hit the space bar, bringing up the report on which Jonathan had been working. I took an extra spin just to convince myself my intentions were honorable. Only when my eye fell on the words *Deadly Harpoonist* did I allow my foot to drag, braking the chair.

Next to the caption was a computer-generated drawing with a picture of a snail exactly like the one in the tank. With its elongated proboscis it had speared a large fish. Under the sketch Jonathan had typed: *"Like the sirens of Greek mythology, venomous cone snails with their brilliantly patterned shells have lured collectors and tourists alike to the coral reefs of the Phillipines, and to the tropical waters off Australia, New Guinea, and the Barrier Reef. With its harpoon like radular tooth, this formidable mollusk can deliver venom so potent, it can immobilize a large fish, which it then reels in and swallows whole."*

There have been times in my life when I've genuinely considered becoming a vegetarian. This was one of them. I envisioned the hapless fish impaled on the end of that line, its body writhing, then stiffening, every instinct programmed for flight, but paralyzed, helpless, as the deadly venom shot through its system.

My eyes dropped to the bottom of the page.

". . . numb feeling starting in the lips and spreading throughout the body. The venom is usually fatal to humans, causing paralysis of the limbs and difficulty in breathing. The pulse becomes thready and rapid, mimicking the symptoms of heart failure. Death occurs from respiratory arrest."

Mimicking the symptoms of heart failure! For an instant my pulse became thready and rapid. I was afraid to get up, afraid I'd fall, but I must have made some sound, because Meg called out to me from the darkroom.

"What'd you say?"

An image played over in my mind—of Jonathan in black diving gear, like some grotesque sea monster stealthily approaching the Machete 42 and tossing one of these deadly creatures into the boat cabin. If Pete, attracted by the beauty of the shell, had gone to pick it up . . .

"There are ways to simulate heart attacks," Ted had said. But what would Jonathan's motive have been? Was he really a mob hit man? A spasm of fear shot through me as I thought of Ted, off guard, alone in the car with him.

Shakily, I got to my feet. Walking was an effort, as though, like my vision of Jonathan, I were swimming underwater. My breath came in short gasps. I knocked on the darkroom door. "Meg," I called, my voice unsteady.

"Hang on. I'm not quite finished."

"Forget the photos. There's something I have to show you."

"Be right out."

I went back to the computer. My eyes kept returning to the phrases *difficulty in breathing, pulse becomes thready and rapid.* I scrolled down. There was something about an omega molecule that sounded sinister, more scientific jargon about extracting the black venom and separating its components.

There were four vials of black viscous fluid in Jonathan's refrigerator!

My eyes devoured the final paragraph.

"On December 16, in compliance with a government directive, I turned over a sample of the venom. My experiments with this toxin are in the preliminary stages, as are those of my fellow marine biologists and neurobiologists. In my opinion, there is no use for this substance other than for control of intractable pain. The consequences of allowing such highly toxic material out of the scientific laboratory, where it might fall into the wrong hands, could be disastrous."

Clever. This article would be published. Jonathan was setting himself up as Mr. Clean should the true cause of Pete's death ever be discovered. No wonder his room contained no personal items. Hit men leave no clues.

I heard the front door open and close quietly. Quickly, I filed the document, my mind racing to invent a logical reason for Meg's and my presence here. I was on my feet, halfway to the darkroom, when I heard a noise in the hallway. Heart thumping, I turned and saw Simon Banion leaning on his umbrella. My initial reaction was giddy relief. I sank back against the wall, panting like an out-of-shape athelete halfway to the finish line. "My God, Simon. You scared me to death."

For the first time since I'd met him, Simon didn't have on his rumpled gray suit or his round rimless glasses. He was wearing a neat tan sport shirt open at the throat, Bermuda shorts, sandals, and dark sunglasses. Even his complexion seemed to have evolved from gray to tan. Everything about him had smoothed out, almost as though someone had run him through a press. He looked ten years younger than the man I'd met on the airplane.

He spoke softly. "When I heard about your little adventure yesterday, I became concerned. Where's Mrs. Reilly?"

I remembered I'd neglected to put the chain on the door, but I knew I'd heard the bolt click when Ted and Jonathan had left. "How'd you get in? The doors were locked."

Banion smiled. "I apologize if my method of entrance was somewhat unorthodox, but I have news that couldn't wait."

"About Kevin?"

"Where's Mrs. Reilly? You'll want to hear this together."

A sick sensation began in my gut. I don't know why I didn't want to tell him Meg was in the darkroom. Maybe it was because he hadn't rung the doorbell before using his "unorthodox method of entrance" or because I couldn't see his eyes behind those dark glasses. Or maybe it had something to do with the fact that I knew Meg could hear everything we were saying, yet she remained silent. Why? Furtively, I glanced up at the red light above the darkroom door.

"She went into town," I heard myself saying, still not sure why I was lying.

"That's odd," Simon's expression was quizzical. "I had an operative watching this house. He saw two men leaving about an hour ago, but he said nothing about Mrs. Reilly."

If he'd had someone watching the house, why was he so concerned about us that he'd felt the need to break in? "She probably went out through the kitchen," I faltered.

Simon strolled over to the computer chair and sat. The screen continued its little screen-saver dance, and my heartbeat kept pace. "I'll wait for her, then," he said.

"Well, if you're going to keep me in suspense till Meg gets back, why don't we at least wait in the living room? There's an aquarium there that—"

"I've seen it."

Did he mean just now or had he been here before?

"We really shouldn't be in Jonathan's room," I persisted. "He's very private about his work—"

"And yet you're here."

"He asked me to feed his snail."

I almost jumped when he laughed. "He did? What did you feed it?"

"Fish food," I said without thinking.

Banion's chuckle sent cold shivers down my spine. He swiveled the chair and snapped his fingers against the tank. Circe waved her harpoon. "My dear Ms. Carlin, do you know what kind of snail this is?"

I tried to recover. "It's a cone-shell snail, but I wasn't about to feed it a live fish. I'll leave that to Jonathan."

"It still looks hungry to me. Why don't we give it one of the fish from the tank in the other room? You might find it enlightening to see what happens to a living creature attacked by a cone snail."

Attempting a smile that failed miserably, my knees buckled and I sank down on the edge of Jonathan's bed. "I don't think Jonathan would appreciate that. Those are pretty expensive fish in there."

"Well, one creature more or less . . ."

Okay. Panic time. If I'd been hooked up to my computer, my fight-or-flight response would've gone off the screen. "How is it you know so much about snails, Simon?" I gulped.

"I learned about this fascinating creature when I was in Australia. I saw a boy die as a result of picking one up to examine the shell. He was dead within an hour. Of course, I'm not an expert like Olsen, though I've learned a great deal from reading his work."

I remembered Francine mentioning the trip. Jonathan's words on the computer swam before my eyes. ". . . in compliance with a government directive . . . turned over a sample of the venom." Could it be . . .

I forced my legs to respond to my brain's command and rose, heading for the door. "I don't know when Meg'll get back. Why don't you stop by later . . . say, around eight?"

"Where is she?" he asked.

Think, Carrie! "Lieutenant Springer phoned. He wanted to talk to her in his office. You know how insistent he can—"

"She went all the way up to Marathon without you?"

"Oh, no. Didn't you know? While he's on this case he's set up a satellite office on Stock Island."

"I thought you said she went into town."

Like I said, my lying skills need honing. I avoided his eyes and hesitated a few seconds too long.

"Well, I meant . . ."

Banion got to his feet. He seemed much taller than he had the other night, or maybe my fear was causing me to shrink. He removed his glasses. His eyes pierced through my skull, seemed to read my thoughts. "I think you're not being straight with me, Ms. Carlin. Why is that?"

"Don't be silly. I have no reason to lie to you." I arranged my features into a pleasant expression and babbled on. "Let's go in the living room. Would you like a drink while we . . ."

My voice trailed off as, from the corner of my eye, I saw his eyes shift upward and take in the red light. Then he had my wrist in a viselike grip and was dragging me across the room to the darkroom. His complexion had turned angry and mottled, almost as red as the light. With his free hand he shook the doorknob. "Come out of there, Mrs. Reilly. I only want the pictures and the negatives. Neither of you will get hurt if you do as I ask. If you refuse, you're putting your friend in grave danger."

"Let go of me!" I jerked my arm free and made a dash for the door, yelling as I ran, "Stay there, Meg! I'll get help!" He caught me by the hair before I'd gotten halfway across the room. I screamed and he smacked me across the head, knocking me onto the computer chair.

"I don't have time for this," he snarled. "Tell your friend to come out."

Tears of pain and humiliation stung my eyes. There was a ringing in my ears. "Go to hell!"

Brandishing the umbrella, he came at me. "Mrs. Reilly," he shouted, "as you've probably figured out from the photographs, I have here a lethal weapon."

A lethal weapon? His *umbrella*? What did he think he was going to do, pummel me to death?

"Cone-snail venom is quite deadly, I assure you. If you want to see your friend alive, I suggest you open the door. You've got just ten seconds."

Cone-snail venom in the umbrella? I was confused, disoriented, Alice in Wonderland—nothing was as it had seemed. Jumbled thoughts raced through my aching head as I tried to jam the puzzle pieces into place. Nothing fit. I made a superhuman effort not to look as terrified as I felt. "Who are you?" I demanded, with all the bravado someone with ringing ears in a life-threatening situation could muster.

He ignored me and started counting. "One, two, three, four . . ."

PERSPIRATION BEADED ON MY forehead and dripped down my face as I sat on the floor leaning against the bed. Meg sat beside me, silent, her hand gripping mine. Simon was between us and the door, standing by the aquarium, Meg's still-wet photographs spread out over the top. The room was so quiet you could hear the leaves of the royal palms rustling.

Finally, he broke the silence. "I do admire your work, Mrs. Reilly. It's too bad you couldn't have gone shopping last Saturday instead of practicing your craft. You've put me in quite an untenable position."

His position was untenable? I licked my lips, trying to unglue them. I took deep breaths and mumbled my focus word, my mantra: *caaalmmm, caaalmmm*. After a few minutes a whiff or two of oxygen penetrated my brain and I started to devise a plan. If I could stall for time, keep him talking till Ted and Jonathan got back or until I could think of some way to incapacitate him, we might have a chance. After all, there were two of us and only one of him. True, he might be carrying a concealed gun, but if his only weapon was the umbrella, between us we might be able to wrest it from him. I itched to get my hands on the pair of heavy bronze dolphin bookends on the shelf over the desk, but they were out of reach. At that moment I would have given all the money in my one remaining mutual fund to have a can of Ruth-Ann's pepper spray tucked inside my bra.

"If you're not FBI," I began, "how come the field office in Miami said you were?"

"Not difficult to arrange."

"Were you ever an agent?"

His brows drew together and he spat his answer. "I spent years working undercover. The Bureau never appreciated the sacrifices I made."

"Is that why you work for the mob now? You weren't appreciated?" I put all the disgust I could manage into the words.

"Now I work for myself." He looked down at me, his expression one of amused disdain. "Don't tell me you swallowed all that Mafia crap."

Regretfully, like a fish caught by Jonathan's cone snail, I had—hook, line, and radular tooth. "You made all that up, then—the story you told me in the restaurant about Pete owing money to the mob?"

"I have no doubt Peter Reilly owed money," he mocked, "but to my knowledge it wasn't to the mob."

"To you? That's why you killed him? Was it drug money?"

"Surely you know there can be other things that motivate people besides greed."

I stared at him blankly. Meg squeezed my hand in mute anguished sympathy.

"Think about the seven deadly sins. Weren't you very recently accused of"—he smiled thinly—"having done away with your husband's fiancée?"

Jealousy. I remembered a thought I'd had earlier. *Cherchez la femme.* "That woman you're with, Francine—"

"Maxine," he corrected.

Maxine . . . Maxie. "Pete's ex-wife! You're having an affair with Pete's ex-wife!"

He laughed. "Not part of the plan. Purely a bonus."

"What plan?"

"The plan for my boat to win the race, of course," he said softly. "Maxine and Stu Kellerman were more than happy to aid me in seeing to it that Peter Reilly and his brother would never enter." He smiled. "For a price, of course. Sadly, not all of us are free from greed."

Maxine and Stu Kellerman. Pete's ex-wife was married to Kellerman, but she was having an affair with Sy Banion. And they'd all been involved in a murder plot! *To win a race?* Preposterous. No one would kill just to win a race. Then I remembered that ice skater, and the lady who planned a murder so her daughter could make cheerleader. I swallowed. "You killed Pete and tried to kill Kevin to get the Machete 42 out of the race? You killed so you could win a boat race?"

"Not just any boat race." His face took on the look of the religious fanatic. "The World Cup."

I felt Meg's body stiffen as we both stared at him, aghast. "And Mrs. Larrabee," I choked. "What did she have to do with anything? Why kill her?"

He shrugged. "She was in the wrong place at the wrong time. She got in the way. Like you."

The philosophy of the psychopath. *One creature more or less* . . . I lost the ability to speak just about the time Meg found her voice.

"You promised to let us go if I gave you the photographs."

"You know I can't do that. If you were a lesser photographer, perhaps . . ."

He held up one of the pictures. Pete had jumped ashore and was bent over tying a line to a cleat on the dock. Banion looked as though he was reaching out to help. Meg had caught him just as the tip of his yellow-striped umbrella jabbed Pete's thigh.

"No one knows I took the pictures. I've never told the police I had the film. Take them, take the negatives. There'll be no proof. We won't say anything."

"I'm afraid I don't believe you."

Silence.

"I want to see my husband again." Meg's voice broke. "I need to know. Is he alive?"

"Oh, didn't I tell you? His walking into the police station accompanined by a black man in dreadlocks about an hour ago is what precipitated my little visit here." He lifted the umbrella and pointed it at Meg. "I do regret I'll have to do you out of your touching reunion."

Meg's a pretty in-control lady, but don't cross the line. Banion just had. Before he knew what was happening, she was on her feet and had landed a vicious karate kick to a very delicate part of the male anatomy. Never again would I tease her about taking tae kwon do. I resolved to sign up if I made it out of this alive. She was a little off center and her sneakers didn't inflict as much damage as a good leather track shoe would have, but Banion howled and dropped the umbrella. Galvanized into action, I went for the bookends, grabbed one, and—turnabout being fair play—aimed straight for his head. It was an almost impossible shot to miss, but as he doubled over, I did, for the second time in my crime-fighting career. The dolphin went crashing into the aquarium. I dodged splinters of glass and the flying contents of the tank as a rush of water cascaded over the floor. It knocked Banion to his knees, but not before he'd delivered a blow to Meg that sent her reeling. I saw him reach again for the umbrella.

"Get back, Carrie!" Meg screamed. "The venom . . ."

Trying to back off, I slid on the wet floor and went down heavily on my butt. Banion was panting, still crouched over in a fair amount of well-deserved agony. He had hold of the handle of the umbrella. I grabbed some nylon and a couple of spokes and held on like a pit bull. We struggled. Under normal circumstances I wouldn't have had a chance in hell pitting my strength against his, but Meg's well-placed kick had weakened him. I was making headway when the spokes broke and suddenly the umbrella tip was aiming straight for my rib cage. I scooted back, made a wild grab for the handle, managed to pull it from his grasp, then almost let go—when my eyes lit on the snail. Harpoon extended, waving like a fishing line searching for prey, it was crawling inch by inexorable inch toward Banion's foot. I started to shout a warning, but some instinct for self-preservation closed my throat. Clinging to the umbrella handle as if my life depended on it—which it certainly did—I watched in fascinated horror as the thing advanced closer and closer to Banion's bare ankle. The harpoon flashed, jabbed into flesh. Banion screamed, his leg jerked sideways, and I ducked as the snail went flying. The umbrella came away in my hands. Clutching it to my chest, I fell back, whacking my head on the chair leg. Everything went blurry.

When my vision cleared and I sat up, the snail was

on its back across the room where Banion had kicked it. Meg, still dazed and clutching her head, was sitting with her back against the door. Banion lay still. His eyes were open, and in them, terror and disbelief were etched for all eternity. A tiny trail of blood was snaking its way from his ankle onto his foot, ending in an obscene puddle on the floor.

There was commotion in the other room—male voices and footsteps. Jonathan's frame filled the doorway, and a thin, bearded Kevin, head bandaged, was cradling Meg in his arms. Then Ted was crouching over me, loosening my hands from the umbrella, and I was struck with an overwhelming sense of déjà vu as, through a fog, I heard him saying, "Let go, Carrie. It's over. You got him. You did it. Let go, sweetheart. It's over."

EPILOGUE

"**I** CAN'T BELIEVE KEV was right here in town with that homeless guy the whole time the police and the Coast Guard were searching for him."

"Joseph Mobutu isn't homeless. He's an artist—has a studio down by Monroe County beach," Ted replied. "Kevin'd lost a lot of blood, was incoherent most of the time. Joseph had no idea who he was."

"It was all over the papers, for God's sake!"

"Joseph doesn't read newspapers. Just be glad he found Kev when he did or he'd've bled to death where he washed ashore."

"Joseph has something against hospitals?"

A deafening roar shattered the peaceful morning as thirty-odd powerboat engines sprang to life. It was Sunday, and we were sitting on the pier in Mallory Square watching the boats in the Open Class as they prepared to follow the red flag being waved by an official on the pace boat.

". . . hasn't much faith in doctors or people in general," Ted was shouting over the din. "Kev had a hard enough time convincing him to get the pin to you."

"Why didn't Kev turn himself in instead of sending Joseph with it?" I yelled into his ear.

He waited till the noise level abated as the boats arrived in the milling area, beginning their five-mile-an-hour counterclockwise circling.

"Too weak. All he could think about was getting a message to Meg."

"All those other messages—the New Year's Eve rendezvous at Christopher House—did Kev have Joseph set that up?"

He shook his head. "All the phone messages were from Banion and the Kellermans, designed to plant the Mafia seed and throw Meg and the police off track. Same thing with the repainted motorcycle that almost knocked you down."

"How did he arrange to have that message at FBI headquarters?"

"He had a buddy in Crenshaw's office route your call through to his old voice mail. To give the guy his due, he didn't know what Banion was up to."

"I still can't comprehend it, that all this was about winning a stupid race."

"That's because you're not a fanatic. Your head's on relatively straight."

A backhanded compliment if ever I'd heard one.

"It was more than ego, though. A lot goes along with a win at a race like this. Big money down the road, a certain life-style. Banion'd worked undercover for four years. It gets to some guys. A few go over the edge."

"Who killed Millie Larrabee?"

"Probably Kellerman, though he hasn't admitted it. He insists Banion hired thugs, but there's no evidence of that."

"What's going to happen to them—Stu and Maxine?"

NANCY TESLER

"At the very least they're accessories to murder." He grinned. "I don't guess they'll be chasing people in cemeteries or doing much of anything other than maybe making license plates—for a long time."

I sighed as my eyes picked out a sleek boat with blue stripes, not unlike Stargazer's Machete 42, crawling just behind the pace boat. The word *Outerlimits* was scrawled across the hull, and from a distance the two young men in the cockpit could have been Kev and Pete. "Kev told me he had the pins made up for himself and Meg— planned to give her hers just before the race," I remarked sadly. "This must be so painful for him. I can't imagine why he wanted to come."

"Closure, I think. A kind of farewell to Pete."

I glanced at Meg and Kevin, who were sitting, arms entwined, several feet away. "It's sad he'll never race again. Meg said he loved it so much."

"Oh, he'll race again."

I pulled back, startled. "You're kidding."

"In his blood. He'll be here next year."

From the pace boat an orange smoke flair shot into the sky, signaling its "three-minutes-to-go" message to the racers below. The pace boat roared away, kicking up a heavy spray, and the flag in the hand of the official changed to yellow. The crowd surged forward, their excitement palpable as the race boats streaked by, cutting through the pace boat's wake. *Like a machete slices through sugar cane,* I thought, and understood why Kev and Pete had chosen the name for the model. Overhead a helicopter hovered, waiting for the first inevitable casualty. I pictured Jonathan in full diving gear, poised to jump into the blackness below. I felt ashamed that I'd suspected him when all he'd been trying to do was to protect Meg

208

and me. Like me, he'd bought into the Mafia's involvement, although his theory had been that Kevin was deeply enmeshed. Generous as usual, despite being half in love with Meg, which I'm pretty sure he is, he'd gallantly offered to move out of his house and bunk with a friend for the rest of the week so Meg and Kev could have his room. Of course, that had allowed Ted to share the little bedroom with me. I'd hardly put up any fight at all.

The yellow flag dropped, was replaced by a green one, the pace boat cut away, and they were off.

"How fast do they go?" I shouted.

"I'd guess anywhere from a hundred to a hundred thirty miles an hour," Ted yelled back.

Banion's offhand remark on the airplane came back to me. "Someone always dies race week in Key West."

"Men and their damned love affair with danger," I muttered. "Poor Meg."

Ted pinned me with his gaze. "She loves him. She'll deal with it."

I knew what that was about, and he wasn't going to get away with it. "What about Kev loving Meg," I demanded, "enough to give up something for her?"

"Men are from Mars, women are from Venus," he quoted, "and that is just the way it is."

"Oh, yeah? Well, it's a darned good thing we Venusians have flytraps in our arsenal," I shot back, "because if memory serves me correctly, last Tuesday the Martians were a little late with the cavalry."

"Slow as snails," he agreed, laughing, and pulled me to him, kissing me tenderly. His hand brushed the still-visible welt on my cheek. "Tell me what I can do to make it up to you."

A warm, fuzzy feeling started in the pit of my stomach, crept its way upward, and settled around my heart. When I could get my breath, I murmured, "Lose the mollusk metaphors. Other than that, I'd say you're definitely on the right track."